"Matt—

"Georgia—

"I was going to apologize. Not for kissing you, because I don't regret it for a moment, but for making you feel uncomfortable."

She didn't regret the kiss, either—just the fact of who he'd been, who he was.

"Come round the farm with me."

"No more kisses?" she challenged, and he smiled, a cockeyed smile that softened the strain in his eyes and made her forget who he was.

"No more kisses," he said, and his voice was full of teasing regret.

"Okay," she found herself saying, and wondered if she was quite mad, or if it was Matt's job to finish sending her round the bend!

Dear Reader,

Do you have the *slightest* idea what we, the authors, subject ourselves to in the name of research? No, I don't mean the love scenes! No, I don't mean delightful, cozy dinners *à deux*. No, I don't mean popping down to London for the Chelsea Flower Show and sniffing roses in a country garden.

I mean *Fear.* Terrifying, paralyzing, mind-numbing fear. Clammy hands. Cold sweat breaking out all over. Adrenaline like you wouldn't believe. Nausea. For days. Invalidation of life insurance.

And why? Because it has to be *Real.* Because, in my infinite wisdom, I decided my hero would take my heroine up in a microlight. Hah! Foolish woman. It's a mistake I won't repeat, and I doubt she will, either! So, dear reader, please do me a favor. If you don't suffer from a fear of heights, if you don't mind sudden, unpredictable movements or handing control of your life to someone you've only just met, don't get motion sick or suffer from panic attacks, spare a thought for those of us who do, and would suffer them anyway, for you, for the sake of authenticity!

I aged ten years the day I went up in a microlight and got to know my weaknesses in intimate detail. I hope you feel it was worth it! Enjoy the book, with my love.

Caroline Anderson

JUST SAY YES!
Caroline Anderson

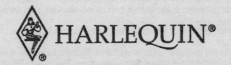

HARLEQUIN®

TORONTO • NEW YORK • LONDON
AMSTERDAM • PARIS • SYDNEY • HAMBURG
STOCKHOLM • ATHENS • TOKYO • MILAN • MADRID
PRAGUE • WARSAW • BUDAPEST • AUCKLAND

ISBN 0-373-03605-1

JUST SAY YES!

First North American Publication 2000.

Copyright © 2000 by Caroline Anderson.

Visit us at www.eHarlequin.com

Printed in U.S.A.

CHAPTER ONE

GEORGIA was exhausted.

She must have walked ten miles round that blasted building site if she'd walked an inch, and if she didn't get her shoes off soon she thought she was probably going to scream.

She dropped her bag on the table, slid her portfolio into the gap between the seats and sat down with a plop. Then with a sigh of relief she kicked off her shoes under cover of the table.

Bliss! She squirmed her toes and sighed again. Thank goodness it was over, she thought, and stared out at the bustle of the railway station, reliving her fruitless and irritating day.

It wouldn't have been as bad if the design hadn't been so far advanced before the client had changed his mind, but no, he'd seen a video of the previous Chelsea Flower Show and been inspired. Could she use more metal? And how about a bigger water feature? Reflective, perhaps—or then maybe not. Perhaps a rill—a little falling stream-let—or better still a waterfall—on a flat site, already horribly over budget!

She'd had her teeth clenched all day so hard her jaws ached. How could the client be so vacillating and still be alive? She would have thought he would have been murdered by now, he was so infuriating!

Still, at least she wouldn't have to speak to him for a few days. Maybe by then she'd have got her temper back—and maybe her hair wouldn't be red any more!

She dropped her head back against the prickly cushion and winced. Damn. Hairclip. She squeezed the wings together and opened the wicked jaws of her favourite clip—the Venus fly-trap, she called it, which, with its vicious teeth, was about the only sort man enough to restrain her wild curls.

She shook her head and they broke free and tumbled down her back. Yet again she sighed with relief, and threading her fingers through her hair, she combed it out roughly, then leant back against the cushion again, comfortable this time. At least she had the little table to herself for a moment. No doubt that state of affairs wouldn't last long, but in the meantime—

She wriggled her feet again, stretched her legs out under the table and propped her heels on the edge of the other seat.

Wonderful. Five minutes like this and she'd stand a chance of feeling human again...

Damn. It was almost full. Still, there was a small table by the window, occupied by a woman with foaming red hair. He chuckled to himself. Occupied, as in taken over completely. A bag as big as a bucket was dominating most of the tabletop, the contents threatening to splurge out—and on the other seat, sticking up like tiny sentinels, were the daintiest, cutest little feet he'd seen in a long time.

She was asleep, her lashes lying in dusky curves on the smooth cream of her cheeks, her mouth soft and rosy and vulnerable. Now in a fairytale, he thought, he would have to wake her with a kiss—

Matthew cleared his throat, pulling himself together. 'Excuse me. Is this seat taken?'

Her lids flew up, revealing wide green eyes hazed with

sleep, and she scrambled back into a sitting position and hooked her feet down, to his disappointment.

'I'm sorry. No—no, I was just stretching out. I must have dozed off. I'm sorry.'

She was embarrassed, dragging the bag towards her and colouring delicately along those rather interesting cheekbones. Her mouth, a little too wide and slightly vulnerable, curved fleetingly into a wry smile as she pushed the bag down at her feet, red hair tumbling wildly around her head.

Matthew squeezed himself into the space between the seat and the table and tried not to fantasise. He put his briefcase down and flipped it open, pulling out the papers he intended to go over again, then snapped the locks shut and slid it behind his legs. Their feet collided, and apologising, they both withdrew to their own sides again.

'There's not much leg-room, is there?' he said, bizarrely conscious of the warm place under his thigh where her feet had been, but she was staring out of the window again, ignoring him.

Just as well. She had a wedding ring on. If she hadn't had, he might have persued the conversation, but it was pointless. Pity. She was rather attractive in a fresh and slightly chaotic sort of way.

He settled down to the papers in front of him, trying unsuccessfully to keep his legs to himself. He had to sit with his knees apart to accommodate hers, and the posture was strangely intimate and made him uneasy.

He hated the train. Given the choice he would have driven, but parking in London was a nightmare.

His phone rang, and he answered it absently, dealt with the call then made another, a follow-on call to clear up some of the unanswered questions, all the time trying not to think about that soft, wide mouth and the firm little knees between his own.

Georgia rested her head against the seat-back, closed her eyes and tried not to let her knees drop against his. It was just too—intimate, really, too personal. Too much.

She shifted in her seat, turning towards the window more, and her knee brushed his again.

They murmured apologies and she shifted back, trying not to eavesdrop on his conversation.

It was impossible not to hear, but it didn't sound all that riveting anyway. Something about political unrest and financial insecurity and government intervention. She looked at him curiously. Arms? Probably plastic document wallets, she thought with a stifled smile—or loo paper.

He had an interesting face but not the face of a criminal. Not conventionally handsome, but somehow attractive. His chin had a little cleft in it, and when he laughed at something the other person said, his eyes creased with humour and she found herself smiling too.

He switched off the phone and put it down, picking up the document on the table and flicking through it, making quick notes in a sharp, jagged hand that fascinated her.

She tried not to stare, but her eyes kept drifting back towards him, to the way the soft lock of hair at the front kept falling forward when he leant over to consult the document. Then he looked up and speared her with those startling ice-blue eyes, and she tried nonchalance for a moment and then dropped her eyes, as guiltily as if she'd been caught with her hand in the biscuit tin.

Out of the corner of her eye she saw his mouth tip in a smile, and colour teased her already warm cheeks.

Damn. By the age of thirty she should have learned to control that childish reaction!

She was relieved when the refreshments trolley was wheeled in and she could find something to busy herself. 'Tea, please. White,' she said, and fumbled for her purse.

The paper cup was set down in front of her, she was parted from an extortionate amount of change, and the trolley moved on.

She saw he'd bought a bar of chocolate and a can of some gaudy tropical carbonated drink that would strip his teeth of their enamel in minutes and do disgusting things to his insides. She shuttered inwardly and stared out of the window again at the advertising hoardings that towered over the grubby little houses, wedged up cheek by jowl against the railway line, crammed with people trapped in the bowels of the dirty city. She could see into their bedrooms—see the unmade bed in one, someone undressing in another. So little privacy.

She closed her eyes. It was too awful to contemplate. How she'd lived in London at all she found quite incredible, even if it had been Knightsbridge. It held no attraction for her at all now, and she couldn't wait until she got home and could wash off the grimy smell and change out of her 'city' clothes into her jeans and soft, baggy old sweatshirt that said 'World's Best Mum' on it in faded white letters.

She thought longingly of a hot bath and a cold glass of Chablis, followed by some light and delicate dish, something clever with fruit and parma ham, seasoned to perfection and exquisitely presented by a discreet and well-trained slave—

In her dreams! It would probably be frozen pizza again, and no doubt that would have to be slotted in round the children's homework, sorting out a load of washing and doing a hundred and one other things that working women did that their spouses thought happened almost by accident.

Not that she had a spouse, not any more, thank goodness. Not for ages, now. Three years. It seemed much longer since her reprieve.

People had commiserated with her when Brian had died, and been puzzled when she hadn't been heartbroken. All except her closest friends, who'd had an inkling of their unhappiness.

Georgia snorted softly. They hadn't known the half of it.

Still, it was over now, over and done with and well behind them. She had a career to be proud of, a lovely house, two gorgeous children that she adored, and the rest of her life to look forward to.

Strange, then, how sitting with her knees between the warm, hard legs of a personable man made her so painfully aware of the emptiness that lingered in the shadows of her crowded and busy life.

She shifted further back on the seat, drawing her legs towards her and away from him, away from temptation and all that wicked sex appeal that she would do well to ignore…

She'd gone to sleep again, her legs falling against his as she relaxed, making him inescapably aware of the soft warmth of her knees pressed against the inside of his thigh.

Still, it gave him a chance to study her without fear of being caught, and as he did so, something teased at the back of his mind. Some occasion when they'd met, but he couldn't place where. She'd been unhappy, though. He could remember those beautiful green eyes welling with tears—and his anger. He remembered the anger, the frustration of not being able to help her, but nothing more.

He tried again, but the memory was too elusive. It was too long ago, too insignificant an event to have registered.

A muffled electronic jingle gradually penetrated his awareness, and Matthew leant forwards and shook her arm gently. 'Excuse me—is that your phone?'

Her eyes flew open and she sat up, her knees withdrawing from his as she scrambled for her bag under the seat. The hideous noise grew louder and she came up flushed and triumphant, phone in hand, and pressed a button, flashing him a smile of thanks that did strange and unexpected things to his heartrate.

'Hello? Joe? Hello, darling. Are you all right?'

Her voice was soft, warm and rich and slightly deeper than he'd expected. A little husky.

Sexy.

Oh, hell. He wondered who Joe was, and tried not to eavesdrop. Fat chance in those close confines. There wasn't much to glean, anyway. It was all trivial household stuff—probably her other half asking the 'What's for supper?' question.

He wondered if she knew how her voice softened as she spoke, and wished he had someone to call who would respond so warmly.

'You're losing it, Fraser' he told himself.

The journey was endless. They sat outside Chelmsford for half an hour, held up by a broken-down train ahead of them, and then finally pulled into Ipswich station three quarters of an hour late.

The train lurched as it came out of the tunnel, sending the dregs of her tea cascading towards her. With a star-

tled shriek she leapt up, swiping wildly at the spreading
stain on her skirt, and he stood up and blotted her with
an immaculate linen handkerchief.

The feel of his hand against her thigh made her blush,
and grabbing the handkerchief from him she gave the
wet patch a couple more swipes and then handed it back.
'Thank you,' she said, kicking herself for sounding
breathless and sixteen and totally out of control.

He smiled, the crinkling of his eyes softening the
strangely icy colour, warming it.

'My pleasure. Are you getting off here?'

She nodded, her feet chasing round under the table
after her shoes, and finally locating them as the train
eased to a much more civilised halt. 'Yes, I am. Oh,
where's my portfolio?'

She pulled it out from between the seats, scooped up
her bag and phone and left, vaguely aware of him following suit in a much more orderly and dignified fash-
ion.

Georgia was past being dignified. Her skirt was
soaked, her feet hurt, her baby-sitter would be edging
towards the door and Joe and Lucy would be vile by
now.

And if her client hadn't fiddled about and changed his
mind for the hundredth time, she would have been on
the earlier train and in the bath by now! She ran down
the platform and over the bridge, out of the doors and
across the road to the car park, fumbling for her keys.

Aha! Finally locating them as she arrived at the car,
she let herself in, started the engine and pulled away into
the evening traffic. Ten minutes and she could have the
wine, if not the bath, the gourmet dinner and the slave!
She whipped round the inner ring road, out into the
country, and was just turning into her lane when an orchestra struck up in her bag.

She stared at it dumbstruck for a second, then pulling over, she rooted about for the source of the noise and came up with her phone.

No, not her phone. *His* phone. Hers absolutely *never* spouted classical music!

She pressed a button and held it cautiously to her ear. 'Hello?'

'Oh—hi. It's Simon here—can I speak to Matt, please?'

She stared at the phone in horror. 'Um—Matt's not here. He's—' Where on earth *was* he? 'Um—he's busy. Can I get him to call you?'

'Sure—he knows the number. Oh, and tell him it's about time.' And with a chuckle, he cut off and left Georgia staring at the phone. With a shrug, she keyed in her own phone number, and waited…

'What the hell?'

A familiar and ghastly electronic jingle erupted from his jacket, and as if it were red-hot, he drew into the side of the road and pulled the phone out of his pocket, staring at it suspiciously. 'Hello?'

'You've got my phone,' her voice said.

He held the thing away from his face and looked at it, blinking. 'I have?' he said. It looked exactly like his own.

'Yes—and I've got yours. They must have got muddled up in the train.'

In the shower of tea, more like. He smiled. 'Ah— apparently. So what are we going to do about it?'

'Well, I can't do anything at the moment,' she said a little crossly. 'I'm already late home and my babysitter will be having kittens. Can you make do with mine until tomorrow?'

'Or I could come to you,' he suggested, wondering at the eagerness he felt surging in him at the thought. She hadn't sounded exactly inviting. 'I expect I'll get all sorts of calls—it'll irritate you to death,' he added, piling on the ammunition.

'Simon already rang,' she told him. 'He said to tell you it's about time, and can you ring him?'

Simon? About time? About time for what? The only thing his friend ever got on to him about was his single status—and a woman had answered his phone. He groaned inwardly and tried again.

'So—shall I come to you?'

'Would you?'

'Sure.' He jotted down the address, noted with interest that it was only a few miles from him along the lanes, and pulling out into the traffic, he changed direction and cut across country towards Henfield. He hadn't had anything else planned for the evening because he'd expected to be in London for longer—it might be rather fun to see where she lived, see if it matched up with the image he had of her.

The word 'babysitter' niggled at him, but he ignored it. She had a wedding ring on anyway, so he knew she was out of reach. That wasn't the point.

He chuckled wryly. He wasn't sure exactly what the point was, but he was almost sure he was wasting his energy thinking about her. If only he could remember more about the first time he'd met her, but he couldn't. He might even have been mistaken, but he doubted it. He didn't usually forget faces or names.

And anyway, he didn't even know her name. Maybe when he did it would fill in the blanks...

'Anna's gone home,' Joe told her, opening the door and scowling at her as she kissed his cheek. 'Jenny's here instead—she said she knew she was early but she's going to help you get ready. Do you *have* to go out again?' he tacked on accusingly.

She stared at her son in horror. 'Go out? I'm not going out!'

'Oh, yes you are. The Hospice Charity auction,' her neighbour reminded her, appearing over Joe's head in the crowded little hall.

Georgia sagged against the door and wailed. 'I'm so tired,' she whimpered. 'I just want a nice cold glass of wine and a little bit of oblivion. Jenny, I can't go!'

'Oh, yes, you can. Go and run the bath, and I'll bring you the glass of wine. You can drink it while you think about what to wear.'

Georgia dropped her folio in the corner of the hall, kicked off her shoes and headed for the stairs. 'Where's Lucy?'

'In the sitting room, asleep. She was tired but she refused to go to bed till she'd seen you in your party dress.'

'Oh, damn,' she said very, very softly, and went upstairs, defeated. Absolutely the last thing she needed was this charity auction, but she'd volunteered her services, and she had to go to be auctioned.

Although why they couldn't just auction her in her absence she couldn't imagine. It was her services they were selling, not her body! Still, they wanted her to go along, so she would go.

She ran the bath, threw in a handful of rejuvenating bath salts, contemplated chucking in the rest of the bag and thought better of it. Since she'd remembered to fill up the water softener, she had enough trouble washing the soap off, without adding to the problem!

Jenny passed a glass of wine through the bathroom door, and she sank into the hot bubbly water, took a gulp of the wine and rested her head against the end. Bliss. If only she could stay there all night...!

Well, he was wrong about the house, anyway. He'd expected a chaotic, colourful little cottage, or a farmhouse down a quiet track. Instead, it was a modest, modern detached house set quietly in Church Lane, and the only thing about it that fitted with his image of her was the garden. It was gorgeous, a riot of unruly colour and texture, a real English cottage garden. That, definitely, was her.

He parked the car, walked up the path to the front door and rang the bell.

'I'll get it,' a voice yelled over thundering footsteps, and the door was yanked open by a young lad of about eight or nine. He had brown hair, mischievous green eyes and the same mouth as his mother. 'Yes?' he said abruptly.

'Um—is your mother in?' Matt felt suddenly foolish. Not knowing her name made him feel awkward, a bit of a charlatan. He held the phone out. 'We got our phones muddled in the train—I arranged to come and swap them.'

'Oh. She's in the bath. You'd better come in. I'll tell her.'

And abandoning the door, he left Matt on the step and ran upstairs. Matt followed as far as the hall, then waited. A small girl appeared, her head topped with a brighter version of her mother's curls, and eyed him curiously, her head tipped on one side as she dangled round the door frame, swinging backwards and forwards like a human gate.

'Hello. I'm Matthew,' he told her. 'I'm here to see your mother.'

She took her thumb out of her mouth and smiled gappily. 'I'm Luthy,' she lisped. 'Mummy'th going out—she'th going to wear a party dreth. I'm thtaying up to thee it.'

Matt worked his way through the lisp to decipher the underlying words, and wondered if he would be able to delay long enough to see Mummy in her party dress, too.

The boy thundered downstairs and skidded to a halt. 'Mum says come and sit down, she'll be out in a minute.'

'Well,' Matt said, 'perhaps your father—'

'He's dead,' they chorused, apparently unmoved.

'Ah.' Matt trailed obediently after them into a scene of utter chaos. The cushions had been taken off the furniture and stacked like a house of cards, to make a sort of den behind the big settee. The chairs had been shoved every which way, and the curtains had been dragged out from the windows to drape over the top, so that they hung at a crazy angle.

'Oops,' said the boy, and grabbing cushions, he began piling them haphazardly onto the furniture. Matt helped, discreetly turning cushions round so the zips were at the back and they went into the right place.

It reminded him of his childhood. How many times had he done that? And how many times had he been skinned for it? He hid a smile and straightened the curtains, just as the woman appeared in the doorway, her hair twisted up in a towel, her feet bare, an ancient towelling robe hastily dragged on and belted with symbolic firmness.

She looked impossibly young to be the mother of these two little scamps—young and vulnerable and freshly scrubbed. His heart beat a slow, steady rhythm, strong and powerful. Lord, she was lovely.

'Hi again,' she said.

'Hi.' His voice sounded rough and scratchy. He tried again. 'Sorry to come at a bad time—'

'That's all right. I'd forgotten I was supposed to be going out.'

'Somewhere nice?' he asked, although it was none of his business, but she wrinkled her nose and shook her head.

'Not really. It's a charity auction for the hospice.'

Guilt prickled at him. He'd been invited and had turned it down because he hadn't expected to be back early enough. Perhaps he ought to go anyway—and he could see her, of course. Not that that had anything to do with why he wanted to go, of course!

'I expect you'll enjoy it,' he said encouragingly, but her nose screwed up again doubtfully.

'Shouldn't think so, it's duty. I'm selling my services.'

His mind boggled. He just hoped to hell what he was thinking didn't show in his eyes, because it was likely to get him arrested.

'What do you do?' he asked, just as the house phone rang.

'Oh—excuse me,' she said, and whirling on her heels, she went into the kitchen and shut the door.

'Mummy duth gardenth,' Lucy told him.

Which explained the riot of colour outside the front door. How useful, he thought, and his mind ran on. A gardener, selling her services at a charity auction—so if he could somehow wangle a ticket at this late stage, he could buy her services in the garden—and several hours of her time. Fascinating.

And she was a widow—not married, and apparently

no man around the place playing the part to get annoyed at his interest.

'So—is Mummy going on her own?' he asked, pumping the children ruthlessly with only the merest prickle of conscience.

'No. Peter'th taking her.'

And who the hell was Peter? 'Peter?' he said guilelessly. Oh, wicked, wicked man to take advantage of their innocence!

'Peter's a friend,' the boy told him flatly, right on cue.

'Joe doethn't like him,' Lucy put in for good measure.

Was Joe another 'friend'?

'So what if I don't? He talks to us like we're idiots,' the boy said defensively. So the Joe she'd been talking to on the phone was her son. Good. One less to worry about—and he didn't like the boyfriend. Even better. An ally.

Then the kitchen door opened abruptly and the woman came back in, the soggy towel in her hand, damp strands of untamed hair clinging to her face and trailing down her shoulders. 'Peter can't make it,' she announced to nobody in particular. 'Damn.'

'Problems?' Matt said, wondering if there was a God after all and if He was about to put such a spectacular opportunity in his lap.

'Yes—my escort for tonight. I really, really don't want to go, but I have to, and I can't think of anything more awful than going on my own. Oh, well, I shall just have to—oh, no!'

Her hand flew to her mouth. 'I've had a glass of wine—I can't drive. Oh, darn it. Taxi—I'll have to call a taxi,' she muttered, thumbing through a tattered phone book.

'I'll take you,' he said without giving himself time to think.

Her head flew up, her eyes widening incredulously.

'You? Why on earth should you do a thing like that?'

He shrugged, wondering what feeble excuse he could come up with that she'd believe, and came up with probably the feeblest.

'Because I muddled up the phones?' he offered. That wouldn't work. She'd taken the wrong phone, not him, and any second now she was going to remember that. He tried again. 'Anyway, didn't you say it was a charity do?'

'Yes—for the hospice, but what of it?'

He shrugged again, trying to look nonchalant when he wanted to punch the air. Yes, there was a God. 'I keep meaning to do something charitable. Here's my chance. I could escort you, so you won't have to go on your own, and you won't have to drive. Simple.' He smiled encouragingly.

She hesitated, for such a long time that he began to lose hope, but then she started to weaken. 'I couldn't possibly let you—'

'Of course you could. I had an invitation to it anyway. Just say yes.'

She wavered, so he pressed her again. 'What time do you need to be there, where is it and what's the dress code?'

She answered mechanically. He could almost hear the cogs in her brain whirring. 'Seven thirty for eight, the Golf Club behind the hospice, black tie.'

'Fine. I'll pick you up at seven.'

'But you'll be bored to death—'

'Rubbish. I might even bid for the odd thing—you couldn't deny the charity the chance to make money out of me, could you?'

'Well…'

He grinned, watching her crumble, and knew he'd done it. Brilliant. 'Do I need to eat first?' he asked, without giving her any further room to wriggle out of it.

She shook her head, looking a trifle shell-shocked. 'No. There's a meal—I've already bought the tickets, so you'll get a free three-course dinner out of it.'

His grin widened. 'Excellent. It's sounding better by the minute. Now, if I could just have my phone—?'

Her hand flew to her mouth. 'Oh, gosh, sorry, I'd forgotten again.'

She went into the hall, her back to him, and rummaged in that amazing bag of hers, giving him an unobstructed view of a curvy and very feminine bottom in faded towelling as she bent over.

'Here it is,' she said, straightening up and turning round, and he dragged in a lungful of air and tried not to look down the gaping cleavage of her dressing gown.

'Thanks,' he said, his voice a little strangled. Their hands touched as they swapped phones, and he was amazed that the sparks weren't visible. 'By the way,' he added with the last remnant of his mind, 'I don't know your name.'

'Georgia,' she said, her voice husky and soft. 'Georgia Beckett.'

Beckett. The memory teased at him, just out of reach. 'Matthew Fraser.' He held out his hand, wondering if he'd survive the contact, and found her slim, work-roughened little fingers firm against the back of his hand. He dropped it reluctantly, stunned by how good it felt.

'Right, I'll see you at seven,' he said.

'I still think it's a dreadful imposition. I could get a taxi, for heaven's sake—!'

'And spend the whole evening on your own? How tedious. Anyway, I'm looking forward to it now. Just go and get ready, like a good girl, and I'll go and harness the chariot.'

She chuckled, a delicious sound that did strange things to him. 'All right,' she said, almost graciously. 'Thank you.'

'My pleasure.' He returned her smile, then pocketing his mobile phone, he let himself out, slid behind the wheel of his car and heaved a sigh of relief.

'Thank you, God,' he said, and couldn't stop himself from laughing out loud as he drove back down Church Lane towards home. He was about to spend the evening with the most tantalizing woman he'd met in ages. If only he could remember why he knew her and where he had met her before...

Georgia sat down on the bottom stair and gazed blankly at the front door. How on earth had she talked herself into that? He could be a mass murderer! His name seemed slightly familiar—from the papers? Perhaps he'd got a prison record? He might have swapped the phones on purpose, as part of some deadly plan to find out where she lived and murder her—

'Oh, Georgia, you've really lost the plot,' she said disgustedly, stomping upstairs. 'Murderer, indeed!' Although he did have disturbingly piercing eyes...

'You're mad,' she told herself, snatching open the wardrobe door and frowning at the contents. 'Now—what is there? Something demure, simple, elegant—what a dazzling choice.'

She took out her black dress—her *only* dress that answered at least some of her criteria—and hung it on the front of the wardrobe. Excellent. Now, shoes, and did she buy a miracle have a decent pair of tights? Glossy, for preference, barely black—

'Aha!' She snatched the new packet victoriously from the drawer, pulled on her underclothes, dried her hair, slapped on a thin layer of light foundation and did something clever with her eyes to widen them a little. Then a streak of lipstick, a quick smack and wriggle of her lips together to spread it evenly, and she was done.

Sucking her lips in so they didn't mark the dress, she shimmied into it, let it settle around her and stood back.

A slash neck, sleeveless but with shoulders that extended to make tiny capped sleeves, it was cut on the cross and fell beautifully to skitter around her ankles, the heavy crêpe moving sensuously as she turned to check the back.

Hmm. She sucked in her stomach, eyed herself again and shrugged. So she was a mother. And anyway, they were selling her design services, not her body, she reminded herself for the umpteenth time. A tiny worm of truth told her that it wasn't the punters at the auction that she was worried about, but the manipulative phone-thief with the cock-eyed grin and the most interesting eyes she'd seen in a long time.

A little flurry of panic rippled through her—or was it anticipation? What on earth had she been thinking about, letting him talk her into this? All that hogwash about depriving the charity of the money he was prepared to spend—dear me, I must be wet behind the ears, she thought in disgust, but she was smiling anyway.

She twirled again, sucking in her tummy muscles, and nodded with satisfaction. She slipped her feet into the shoes, winced at the thought of standing for hours on feet that had already done a marathon day, and humming slightly under her breath, she went downstairs.

Jenny said, 'Wow!', Lucy hugged her and said she was beautiful, and Joe said, 'Go, Ma!'

Approval? Heavens!

Now, all she needed was her escort…

CHAPTER TWO

IT WAS a glittery do, sprinkled with rich women in mahogany tans and diamonds and not much else, and paunchy men glistening in the heat, their ample middles girdled up in cummerbunds to hide the fact that their trousers were too tight after dinner.

Still, they were rich, they were going to spend their money in a good cause, and Georgia was just only too glad she was no longer part of that scene. She'd hated it—hated the entertaining for Brian's clients, hated the strain and pressure he'd put her under, hated the false smiles and backstabbing bonhomie.

Matthew, on the other hand, seemed to fit right in, except that his dress suit fitted him to perfection, gliding over his broad shoulders and tapering elegantly to his narrow waist and neat hips. The shirt was stark white against his skin, and she would lay odds his bow tie was a real one, not a cheat on a bit of elastic.

He wasn't sweating, either, and he looked comfortable and at ease talking to his numerous acquaintances. They'd been seated together at dinner, but she'd been monopolised by the man on her other side, and she'd hardly had a chance to talk to him.

Pity, but maybe a good thing. He was altogether too interesting for her peace of mind, and when he bent his head closer to some clinging little vine to hear her doubtless inane conversation, Georgia found herself smitten by a wild urge to club him over the head with the nearest chair.

Jealousy? Good grief! It was years since she'd felt *anything*, never mind jealousy! And over a total stranger! How perverse.

How worrying…

'Georgia, my dear, you're looking lovely!'

'Thank you, Adrian. You're too kind.' She looked up into Adrian Hooper's slightly glazed eyes and dredged up a smile.

He was the organiser of this shindig, a mover and shaker in local commerce, and she had a lot of respect for him. Unfortunately, he fancied her and it definitely wasn't mutual. She deftly changed the subject. 'It's a good turn-out tonight—all the wallets bulging, I hope?'

He laughed. 'One can only hope so, my dear.' He edged closer, a conspiratorial glint in his eye. 'By the way, was that Matthew Fraser I saw you with earlier?'

She was intrigued. 'Yes—why, do you know him?'

He threw back his head and laughed. 'Of course I know him. Heavens, darling girl, everyone knows him! He's—'

'Adrian, old man, you're hogging all the talent. Aren't you going to introduce me?'

Georgia's heart sank. Adrian she could cope with, but this man was trying to see through her clothes and it was frankly a little embarrassing. Anyway, she wanted to hear more about Matthew—

'Tim Godbold,' the man said, sticking out his hand so Georgia had no option but to take it. 'And you're the famous Georgia Beckett. My dear, I'm delighted to meet you. Such talent as yours is rare indeed.'

'You're too kind,' she said, scraping together a bright smile and wondering when he was going to release her hand from his damp and limpid grip. She eased it away and leant on the table behind her, discreetly wiping her palm on the heavy damask tablecloth. Yuck.

'So what are you here for tonight, Mr Godbold?' she asked, steering attention back to him.

'Tim, please,' he demurred with a laugh that she could only describe as intimate. Oh, Lord, she was going to be ill.

'Tim,' she said with a sickly grin. 'What are you bidding for?'

Big mistake.

'Besides you, of course,' he said with that husky possessive laugh again, and looked around, 'perhaps the membership of the Golf Club—I never play, but it's a good club, I hear. And maybe the car valet, or the weekend for two in the hydro—if I could persuade someone to come with me, of course...'

Georgia, glass to her lips, took a gulp of wine by accident and began to cough. Another mistake. Tim Godbold's damp and heavy hand descended on her shoulderblades with a possessive and intimate pat, totally ineffectual and utterly unnecessary. She waved him away, lost for words, and looked wildly around for a distraction.

Adrian had wandered off, doing his fundraiser's bit, and Matthew was nowhere to be seen. Blast.

Help, though, was at hand. Mrs Brooks, the chairman of the charity, stood up and called everyone's attention to the auction which was about to begin.

Georgia, hugely relieved and almost able to speak again, excused herself and went over to the podium, in case she was asked to explain what she was offering, but in the end she didn't need to explain anything.

The auctioneer had been well primed. He banged his gavel to get everyone's attention, launched into the sale and achieved some staggering sums for really quite silly things.

Then he reached the climax of his patter. 'Ladies and gentlemen, now we come to our star prize of the evening. She's a nationally renowned garden designer, she's been invited by the Royal Horticultural Society to exhibit a show garden at the Chelsea Flower Show next year, and she's very kindly offered a day of her most valuable time to help you realise the garden of your dreams.

'She's more than qualified to design anything from a roof garden to a motorway service area, but her forte is the restoration of historic gardens—'

Out of the corner of her eye, Georgia saw Matt Fraser's body straighten. She caught his eye, speculative and searching, and looked away—straight into the even more speculative eyes of Tim Godbold. He'd threatened to bid for her. Oh, Lord. She started to feel slightly sick.

'And, of course, as it's only April now there's still plenty of time to get plants in and start seeing the fruits of your labours this summer, so come on, ladies and gentlemen, what will you bid me for a day in the company of the gorgeous Georgia Beckett?'

The bidding started at a nice sensible figure—nothing like what she charged for a day's consultation in a garden, but enough as an opening bid. Then it started to rise, steadily at first, and then by larger increments. The other bidders dropped out one by one, and she watched in fascinated horror as Tim Godbold and Matthew Fraser battled for her across the room.

It was like some ghastly game of dare, she thought, each one throwing down a more outrageous bid, each determined to win. She hardly dared to look at them,

Tim glassy-eyed and sweating slightly, Matthew with a grim line to his mouth that brooked no argument.

By the time it reached four times the real cost of her day's work, she was getting distinctly uncomfortable. She was happy for the charity, but even so! It was only one day, for heaven's sake! No designs on paper, no planting schemes—just a wander round and a quick chat, in essence. So what were the two men bidding for?

Then Matthew spoke up, cutting through the auctioneer with his strong, clear voice, throwing down his final bid like a gauntlet.

There was a ripple of shocked delight through the crowd, and all eyes swivelled to Tim Godbold. He dithered for a moment, then threw down his programme and stalked off.

She thought he was going to blow a fuse. She was certain she was. She closed her eyes, wondering if anyone actually *did* die of humiliation, and heard the auctioneer say, 'Going once, going twice, *sold* to Mr Fraser.' The gavel smacked down on the desk with a victorious thunk, and wild applause broke out.

'My God, it *is* a slave auction,' she muttered under her breath, and forced herself to open her eyes and smile vacantly at everyone.

Then Matt was at her side, taking her arm possessively and smiling down at her as if he'd bought her and not just eight hours of her time. He looked disgustingly pleased with himself, and she felt sick and more than a little angry.

She yanked her arm away. 'What the hell was that little exhibition about?' she stormed under her breath. 'Wrangling over me like a couple of dogs over a—a—!'

He opened his mouth to speak, and she skewered him with a glare. 'Don't even think it,' she growled.

'I was going to say bone,' he said mildly, and grinned. 'Anyway, you should thank me.'

'Thank you? Thank you! Are you mad? I thought I was going to die of embarrassment!'

'Nonsense. Anyway, would you rather I'd let Tim Godbold get his sticky little paws on you?'

'Maybe,' she said unreasonably, trying not to shudder. 'Perhaps he's got a genuine need for a garden designer.'

He bent his head closer. 'And perhaps he had his garden landscaped last year at enormous expense—rumour has it six figures.'

Her jaw dropped, and she snapped her mouth shut and looked away. 'Oh.'

'Yes, oh. And, for your information, I have a need. A very genuine need which I think you're perfectly qualified to meet.'

Why did she get the feeling he wasn't talking about gardens?

'We'll see,' she said, and felt a little shiver of anticipation in amongst the rage. She'd been secretly hoping that the day she'd donated would lead to further work. Now she was wondering just what she'd let herself in for! Still, it could have been worse. It could have been Tim Godbold, she thought, and shuddered.

What was that expression the Victorians had used? A Fate Worse Than Death?

Yes. Matt Fraser, for all his faults, *had* to be better than that!

She was still bristling with temper, Matt realised. Oh, well. If he'd hoped for gratitude he was clearly doomed to be frustrated, but that was just too bad. He hadn't liked the way Godbold was looking at her, not at all.

Had she heard the rumours about him? Probably not. A band struck up, and he turned to her with a smile, mouth opening to ask her for a dance, but she didn't give him the opportunity.

'I'd like to go home, please,' she said, in a quiet voice that brooked no argument.

That suited Matt. He'd had a long day, and frankly if it hadn't been for the enticing thought of holding Georgia in his arms, he would cheerfully have left the moment he'd written out his cheque.

'Fine,' he said, and started to manoeuvre them towards the door.

However they weren't to get away with it. Mrs Brooks came sailing up with a big smile. 'Georgia, darling, thank you! What a star! And Matthew—how kind of you to be so generous yet again, and after you said you couldn't come, you naughty man! Now, you can do one thing more for me—start the dancing off, *please*.'

'Just one, for the charity?' Matt murmured to Georgia, and with a little sigh she smiled graciously at Mrs Brooks.

'Just one, for the charity,' she echoed, 'and then I must go. I've been on site in London all day and I'm bushed.'

'Bless you, darlings. And thanks again.'

She sailed off, another victim in her sights, and Matt turned to Georgia with a wry smile. 'You could try not to look as if I'm going to murder you later,' he teased, and she snorted softly.

'How do I know you're not?'

He chuckled. 'You'll have to trust me.'

'Little Red Riding Hood made that mistake with the wolf, if I remember correctly. How big are your teeth?'

He bared them in a mock snarl, and she laughed, for the first time. Catching her in a weak moment, as it were, he took her gently by the arm and led her onto the dance floor, then bowed his head, a slight smile still playing round his lips.

'Shall we dance?'

It was torture. Her body was soft yet firm, her back under his hand strong and straight, yet with the supple grace of an athlete. She held herself away from him a fraction, and he didn't push it. Instead he held her lightly, waiting for the moment when the soft lights and romantic music made her weaken.

Others joined them, and someone bumped into them, jogging her against him so that her soft, full breasts pillowed gently against his chest. For a moment she resisted, then with a tiny sigh she settled against him. He nearly trod on her then, because she felt so good, so soft and warm and feminine, that he thought he would make an idiot of himself.

He'd never held her before. Wherever they'd met, under whatever circumstances, he would have remembered if he'd held her...

Then the music stopped, and with what could almost have been reluctance, she moved out of his arms.

'Can we go now?' she said, and he realised she'd just been leaning on him because she was tired. It was in her voice, in her eyes, in her whole body.

'Of course.' He retrieved her jacket from the cloakroom attendant, settled it round her shoulders and swept her quickly past all the people who suddenly wanted to talk to her.

Then he ushered her to his car and slid behind the

wheel, pausing as he clicked his seat belt into place to study her face in the dim glow of the interior light.

'You're still mad with me,' he said, just as the light faded down and switched off so that he couldn't see her face. She didn't reply, just sat there, staring straight ahead. He thought she was frowning.

Ah, well. He started the engine and pulled slowly out of the car park, heading for Henfield. She was silent for a few taut minutes, during which he could hear her brain working overtime—searching for the right acidic put-down, no doubt. Then suddenly she spoke, her voice quiet but full of suppressed emotion.

'What do you want with me?' she asked tightly. 'I don't even know who you are, and you start throwing around outrageous amounts of money for eight hours of me telling you what perennials to put in where!'

'Don't you mean telling me where to put them?'

She laughed, a brief gust of cynical humour which was quickly suppressed. 'Whatever. I just felt embarrassed by the bidding—it all seemed to get suddenly very personal. I began to feel like a—a trophy or something.'

'How perceptive of you,' he said softly, and out of the corner of his eye he saw her head swivel towards him. 'Tim Godbold wanted you. He wanted to be able to say he'd had his garden landscaped by a Chelsea designer. And he had a more personal interest.'

'Personal?' she said coldly.

'Yeah, personal. You know. Oh, come on, Georgia, don't be naive! He's not a nice man.'

'I noticed.'

'He has a reputation. There are rumours.'

'Rumours?'

'An attempted rape case. It was dropped—and the victim suddenly started spending rather a lot of money.'

She went very still. 'He bought her silence?'

'There was no proof. It just seemed a rather strange coincidence.'

She was quiet for a long while, and then with what seemed to him either utter foolishness or a great deal of courage, she turned towards him again and said, 'And you? Are you a nice man? Or are you just a little more discreet?'

He laughed softly. 'Both. And I really do need your help with my garden. But just to set the record straight, yes, I do have a personal interest in you—I think you're fascinating, and I'd like to get to know you better. It's up to you what you want to do about it. Unlike Tim Godbold, I'm actually going to give you a choice.'

She snorted softly. 'And I suppose I should be grateful.'

'Don't force yourself.' He felt a prickle of irritation. He'd just spent an outrageous amount of money to rescue her from that slimy toad, and if he'd been expecting gratitude, he was obviously not going to get it.

He turned into her drive, cut the engine and looked across at her in the harsh glare of her outside light, his irritation growing. 'Look, forget anything personal. You owe me a day in the garden. I suggest for both our sakes we get it over with as quickly as possible.'

She stiffened, drawing in a quick breath as if he'd hurt her feelings. Good. About time. She'd given his a fair old battering. 'OK. When do you want me to look at it?'

'Did you have a date in mind?'

'Well—this week or next I'd earmarked for it, really.'

'Tomorrow?'

'Oh! But—I haven't got a babysitter—'

'Well, if there's no alternative you'll have to bring them with you. There are plenty of people kicking about at home who can entertain them if need be.' He crossed his fingers, hoping Mrs Hodges wouldn't have decided to go to town for the day with her daughter.

'I don't even know where you live,' she said.

'Heveling—it's easy to find. Here—have a card.'

He pressed it into her hand, all thoughts of kissing her goodnight now flying out of the window along with his tenuous grip on his temper. He leant across instead and pushed open her door. 'What time tomorrow?'

'Um—nine?'

'Fine.'

She looked at him blankly for a moment, then gave him a wary smile. 'OK. And you're sure it's all right to bring the children?'

'Sure.'

'OK.' She got out of the car and paused, obviously struggling with her better nature, then gave him a wry grin. 'Thanks for tonight.'

He snorted, but chivalry prevented him from driving off until he'd seen her close the front door behind her, then he reversed carefully off her drive and went home.

At least the dog would be pleased to see him!

'Well?' Jenny said, studying her with avid interest. 'Did they sell you?'

Georgia laughed wryly. 'Did they ever. Jenny, I thought I was going to die. This awful, slimy man and Matthew started bidding for me against each other. I was so embarrassed.'

'Oh, my goodness. Did it get all terribly personal?'

'Just a bit. Tim Godbold was all but drooling—'

'Tim Godbold! Not *the* Tim Godbold?''

Georgia groaned. 'Probably. Don't tell me you've heard of him?'

'Well of course I have! It was all over the papers! He tried to rape that girl—a temp working in his office. Made her work late and tried it on. It all fell flat because she suddenly decided not to testify.'

Which backed up Matt's story. She suddenly began to feel very grateful to him. 'Anyway, Matt won, and I'm going to look at his garden tomorrow,' she said, and glanced down at the card in her hand.

Her eyes widened, and she realised her mouth was hanging open. She snapped it shut, closed her eyes and opened them again. 'Oh, Lord,' she said weakly.

'What? What is it?'

'He lives at Heveling Hall,' she told Jenny. 'That must be why his name seemed familiar. Oh, blast. He lives at my favourite house in the whole world, and he wants me to tell him what to do with the garden!'

'Well, that's great,' Jenny said, beaming. 'Isn't it?'

Georgia thought over all the horrible things she'd said to him, and what she'd since found out about Tim Godbold, and felt sick.

'I hope so,' she murmured. 'I may, on the other hand, have just thrown away the opportunity of a lifetime.'

Saturday dawned bright and clear, a lovely mid-April day. She woke the children at eight, told them they were going out for the day to Matthew's house and was greeted with howls of protest.

'I wanted to play with Tom!' Joe wailed. 'We were going to play football!'

'An' you thaid Emily could come!' Lucy added, bursting into tears.

Oh, Lord, who'd be a mother? 'Listen, kids, it's OK. You'll love it. He lives at Heveling Hall.'

The noise ceased abruptly. 'Heavenly Hall? Really?' Joe said, eyes wide. Lucy for once was speechless.

'Really,' Georgia told them. 'So come on, let's have you up and dressed and having breakfast in ten minutes, please. I don't want to be late.'

She left them rushing about searching for their clothes, and went downstairs. She had to check her post and pay a couple of bills. Doing that left her rather short for the month, and although she had all the kudos of the Chelsea Flower Show coming up, preparing for it was going to take a humungous amount of time and effort—and while she was worrying about that, she couldn't be earning money on normal commissions.

And now, because Matt Fraser had bid so much for her, she felt morally obliged to give him more time than had been agreed, even though her initial reaction had been to tell him to take a flying leap and to reimburse him.

Good job she hadn't followed up on that one! She simply didn't have enough money in the world to pay him back for that grand gesture.

Oh, well, no doubt he could afford it.

The children came flying downstairs, laces undone, hair unbrushed, eyes wide. 'Doeth he really live at Heavenly Hall?' Lucy asked excitedly. 'Really, truly?'

'Really, truly. Here—this is his card.'

She showed the children the card Matt had given her last night, and Lucy, whose reading was not getting off to a tremendous start, waded through the words laboriously. 'Wow,' she whispered, awed.

'Come on, breakfast,' Georgia said, taking the card back and filing it in her purse. 'We need to go.'

He was right, it was easy to find—particularly if you often took this detour in order to drool over it, Georgia thought. The children called it Heavenly Hall because when she was younger Lucy hadn't been able to remember Heveling, and it had become their pet name for it.

Well-named, to boot. It was gorgeous, soft and mellow and beautiful, and Georgia's hands against the steering wheel felt prickly with anticipation.

And now she was doing what she'd never thought to do, turning onto the drive with its pretty cast iron bridge, crossing the little river that bordered the road and going up the gravel sweep to the side of the house.

The children tumbled out of the car, excited and yet over-awed all at once, and Georgia followed more slowly, her eyes scanning the building hungrily.

Soft rose-pink bricks, mellow with age, soared up towards the sky, punctuated by the gleaming white of freshly painted windows. An ancient wisteria clothed the end wall nearest her, its drooping pale lilac panicles and bright green leaves in gentle contrast to the smothered wall. Old urns spilling over with ivy bracketed the steps leading to the door, and with one last glance round she called the children to her side and rang the bell.

A huge cacophony of noise erupted on the other side, and she heard a firm command and the noise subsided to a whine. Then the door swung open and Matt stood there, dressed in jeans and a freshly pressed white shirt, looking younger and sexier and more edible than a man had any right to look.

Georgia struggled for something sane to say, but it wasn't necessary, because by this time the children had met the dog and were in raptures.

She eyed it a little worriedly. 'It is all right, I take it?'

A hand dropped onto the dog's shaggy grey head, just

by his hip, and Matt smiled. 'He's a pussy-cat. His name's Murphy. He's an Irish wolfhound.'

'To keep you in order—how appropriate,' Georgia said without thinking, and he tipped back his head in the sunlight and laughed.

'Come on in—I'm having breakfast. Join me. Have you eaten?'

'Yes,' she told him.

'But we're still hungry,' Joe said hopefully.

'Joe!'

'Only a bit,' Lucy added diplomatically, but Matt didn't seem worried.

'Come on, then. Don't want the toast to get cold.' And he led them down the hall, past doors Georgia was dying to stick her head round, and into a big, bright kitchen at the back of the house.

It was clearly a work in progress. Wires dangled here and there, the walls were patched and filled, and frankly it was a mess. Most people would have pulled out all the old cupboards and refitted it in an instant.

Georgia thought it was lovely just as it was, with its mismatched units and chipped white butler's sink, because it had a huge table in the middle of the floor, with a pile of newspapers, toast, butter and so forth at one end and a fat ginger cat curled up on it at the other.

Georgia would have given her eye-teeth for a table like that.

For *room* to have a table like that, for heaven's sake!

Lucy rushed straight for the cat and mauled it, and the cat, to its eternal credit, did nothing in retaliation, but simply began to purr ecstatically.

'Coffee?' Matt said, brandishing the pot, and a fragrant aroma of real, fresh coffee wafted towards her. She nearly drooled.

'Thanks. I never get round to making real coffee,' she confessed.

'I only do at the weekends, but something has to be sacred.'

He smiled, his eyes crinkling at the corners, and she began to relax. Maybe she'd imagined his bad temper last night.

But she hadn't. He settled the children down on chairs with toast and homemade jam, and handed Georgia her coffee, holding onto the mug as she took it.

She looked up at him and met his eyes, thoughtful and tinged with what looked like regret.

'About last night—I'm sorry things got off to a bad start. Can we try again?'

Relief flooded her—though whether relief at having another chance at a restoration project to die for, or at having another chance with Matt, she wasn't sure.

She didn't dare analyse it. She simply smiled. 'That sounds good,' she murmured, and with a wink he released the coffee and turned away, just in time to see the ginger cat licking a huge lump of butter off the edge of Lucy's toast.

'Scally, you wicked cat,' he scolded, and scooped the cat off the table. It yowled in protest, but he put it out of the back door and shut it again firmly. 'He's such a thief. Let me get you more toast,' he said, taking the licked piece out of Lucy's hand and slinging it in the bin.

'I didn't mind,' Lucy said, slightly wide-eyed. 'I like Thcally.'

'And I'm sure he likes you—especially when you let him share your breakfast—but he's too fat. He's supposed to be outside catching mice, not in here stealing butter.'

Georgia stifled a smile and watched Matt dealing with the children. He seemed a natural with them, and she wondered if he had any of his own—perhaps living with an ex-wife?

The thought gave her a strange pang of something she didn't care to analyse. It was much too soon in their relationship to have pangs of anything!

A woman bustled in and was greeted with enthusiasm by the dog, tail and tongue lashing furiously. 'Oh, Murphy, stop it,' she said affectionately, scrubbing her spitty arm on her skirt. 'Right, Matthew, what did you want me to do?'

'Entertain the troops. I think food should do the trick for a minute, but then I'll leave it up to you. Georgia, this is Mrs Hodges. She's my housekeeper. Mrs Hodges, this is Mrs Beckett, and these are her children Joe and Lucy.'

Georgia looked at the pleasant-faced, maternal woman greeting her children with a smile, and felt relieved. She looked as if she could cope easily with two youngsters for a couple of hours, and that meant she could go and get on with what she was here for—namely that gorgeous garden.

'Shall we take our coffee and wander round? Then I can tell you what I know as we go.'

'Sure.' She stood up, scooping up her mug, and followed him.

He didn't go outside, to her surprise, but led her out into the hall, and up a graceful, curving staircase to the upper floor. What on earth is he doing? she thought with a little flutter of panic.

He reached a door, stretching his hand out for the knob, and she thought again of that Fate Worse Than Death. Oh, my God, he's going to take me into his bedroom and seduce me while his housekeeper looks after my children! she thought with a hysterical giggle bubbling in the back of her throat.

Then he threw open the door and led her into the remains of an elegant drawing room, shabby now and tired but once glorious, and paused in front of a great mullioned window overlooking the garden.

'That's the problem,' he said thoughtfully.

Georgia marshalled her hysterical and somewhat crazy brain, and peered down into—nothing.

A walled garden, almost square, with an area of flat and tatty grass interrupted by molehills and thistles, and around the edges the straggling remains of a rose garden almost totally submerged in weeds.

'That,' he said deadpan, 'is a formal parterre.'

She lost it. The giggle fought its way up, battling all the way, and erupted in a shower of sound that echoed round the room and left her feeling silly.

Until she saw his smile. 'You see my problem? You see why I needed you? Especially when I found out that the restoration of historic gardens was your forte.'

Georgia looked again, and in her mind's eye she could see the outline of an old knot garden, neat little hedges arranged in complicated and stylised knots with spaces filled with scented herbs. Designed to be viewed from above, the intricate and lovely garden had been long stripped out and destroyed.

She stared again at the unkempt grass. 'Restoration?' she said weakly.

He shrugged and smiled. 'Perhaps recreation would be a more appropriate word. Come on—I'm going to take you a bit higher, so you get a better look.'

And he turned and retraced his steps.

'You're going down,' she said, confused.

He threw a grin back over his shoulder. 'Only for a moment. Then we go right up.'

Even more confused, she followed him. He went via the kitchen, putting his mug down on the draining board. There was no sign of the children or Mrs Hodges or the dog, she thought absently, trailing after him into the sunshine and across a courtyard to a cluster of farm buildings.

Perhaps they were going to climb a grain hopper, she thought, but there wasn't one, and he was heading for a barn—just an ordinary, big black Suffolk barn. She was more puzzled than ever. Whatever was he doing?

Then he flicked a catch, dropped his shoulder against the edge of a huge sliding door in the side of the barn and pushed, and Georgia, who absolutely definitely didn't like heights, felt suddenly terribly uneasy...

CHAPTER THREE

'WHAT'S that?' she asked, her voice a reedy squeak.

'A microlight.' He threw a grin over his shoulder. 'I said we'd go right up!'

Georgia could only stare, frozen, at the gleaming little toy in front of her.

Admittedly it was a heck of a toy—a rich boy's toy, the sort of thing her late husband would have loved had he ever been sober long enough to take his pilot's licence. She wasn't afraid. There was no need to be afraid, there was no way she was going anywhere near it with the engine running.

It looked like a tiny, gleaming little plane from the front, its shiny, smoothly curved nose pointing up into the air, a wheel dangling underneath it. There was a little tube sticking out of the nose, and she pointed to it. 'What's that?'

'Measures the air speed,' he told her over his shoulder. He was looking at something behind the wings. She followed him round and continued her inspection. A curvy canopy, perspex or somesuch, arched over the cockpit, if that wasn't too grand a word, and inside it bristled with all sorts of dials and switches and sticks with padded grips on—joysticks?

Joy? Ha-ha. And where on earth were you supposed to put your legs, even supposing you were fool enough to get in it? She carried on round, and came to a grinding halt.

'Where's the back?' she asked, and he chuckled,

ducking back under the wing and lolling, ankles crossed, against the fuselage.

Fuselage? Far too big a word for this little torpedo-sized coffin.

'It doesn't have a back,' he told her confidently. 'That's it.'

'That tiny pod, two wings and a bit sticking out the back with a waggly thing on it—that's *it*?' she said incredulously. 'Where's the engine?'

'Here.'

He ducked under the wing again and led her round to the back. There, bolted onto the rear of the cockpit and looking for all the world like an optional extra, was an engine, exposed to the elements, no cover, no cowling or anything like that, just the engine sitting there with a propeller hanging off the back of it, too flimsy for words.

'Why isn't it covered?' she asked in amazement.

'No need. And anyway,' he said with a cheeky grin, 'it's sort of sexy to have your engine on the outside. Hunkier. More macho.'

She snorted. Sexy, indeed. 'What's it all made of?' she asked, tapping experimentally on a wing.

'Styrofoam, thin ply, aluminium and fabric, mostly.'

She closed her eyes. Those nasty foam cups you bought tea in at shows were Styrofoam. It was made of plastic cups and bits of material, for heaven's sake, held together with a bit of flimsy aluminium and a veneer of wood to give it the appearance of solidity!

Great.

'And you go up in this thing?' she asked in amazement.

He laughed. 'It's brilliant—it's really fun. You'll love it.'

Fear clawed at her, and she shook her head vigorously. 'Oh, no, I won't love it. No way. Not a chance.'

'It's very safe—trust me. There have been no crashes due to manufacturing or equipment failure in the whole history of its production. It can't stall, either—it just won't do it.'

'They said all sorts of things about the *Titanic*, as I remember,' Georgia said drily.

He shook his head reprovingly. 'Oh, ye of little faith. I'll get it out and you can just sit in it and pretend.'

'Hmm.'

He grinned, that lazy boyish grin that made him look years younger and infinitely sexy, then shouldering the bit that looked like a dragonfly's tail, he straightened easily, then pushed the machine carefully out through the huge opening in the side of the barn.

It looked even smaller outside, against the side of the barn and next to a big four-wheel drive that towered over it like a monolith.

He flipped a couple of catches on the cockpit canopy and unhinged it, so it was open to the elements, then he held the nose down with his hand. 'Hop in, have a feel,' he said with that wretched grin again.

She did, finding that her feet barely reached the pedals. He told her what all the dials were and what they did, and then told her to get out and climb into the back.

'Why?' she asked suspiciously.

'Trust me. I have to do pre-flight checks and put some fuel in. It'll take a moment. You might as well try out the passenger bit while you wait, and it'll help me because you'll hold the nose down so I can get more fuel in. Don't want to run out.'

Indeed not. So she climbed out of the front, and squirmed and squiggled her way into the back seat, and discovered another set of controls—waggly bits under her feet and joysticks and so forth. It was much more cramped than the front, but still bigger than she'd imagined from looking in.

Claustrophobic, though. There was a tiny little circular thing in the perspex, a vent, she imagined. Too small a hole to climb out of if you changed your mind, she thought with a touch of hysteria. Still, it didn't matter. She wasn't going anywhere.

She fiddled about with the controls, touching them cautiously, and then suddenly the joystick moved and she jumped and gave a little shriek.

'It's OK, I'm just checking the rudder and the flaps. Don't panic,' he said from behind her.

Then he ducked under the wing and stood beside her, grinning again. It didn't fool her for a moment. 'How about a little flight?' he said coaxingly. 'Just up, round the house and back down, if you like. Nothing too fancy. The weather conditions are perfect, and the wind direction is excellent for the runway.'

She studied his eyes—honest, sincere eyes, no trickery, except for that grin—and decided she did trust him. Ish. Adrenaline rushed through her.

'Just round the house and down?'

He nodded. 'We have headphones so we can speak to each other—you can tell me if you hate it and we can come straight back down, and if you love it, we can go further.'

'I'm a single parent,' she reminded him, her heart beating with anticipation and dread in equal part.

'I know,' he said calmly. 'Trust me, I don't have a death wish. It's as safe as it's possible to be.'

Georgia didn't doubt it. She just didn't think it was

possible for anything built out of plastic cups and kite fabric to *be* safe!

'Just a very short flight,' she agreed, wondering if she'd totally taken leave of her senses.

It seemed to make him happy, though. He winked, told her how to strap herself in, showed her how the headphones worked and then closed her canopy and hopped into the cockpit. 'Can you hear me?' he asked, adjusting the headphones.

'Yes. It's fine.'

'Right, I'm going to start the engine—it'll be loud, and a bit rough for a moment or two, then it'll settle.'

He was right, it was loud. Very loud, and screwed to her shoulderblades. She could feel the thing thrashing right behind her, and just hoped it was bolted to the body securely.

Then they started to move, taxiing slowly across the concrete apron and over to a wide strip of grass. It didn't look hugely long for a runway, but then she supposed it wasn't a commercial jet, so it probably didn't need to be very long.

That was her last conscious thought.

The revs picked up, the little plane juddered for a moment, then started to run forwards over the grass, steadily accelerating. She could feel the ground bumping rapidly under her, then suddenly the bumps were gone, and a second later the horizon skidded out underneath her and she felt as if she was headed straight up into the ether.

She screamed, gripping the struts above her like grim death, and Matt reached for the volume control on the side of his headphones and adjusted it.

'Are you all right?' he asked, and she heard him, astonishingly, over the racket of the engine. He felt very close—comfortingly so, because she was trying very hard not to look down and was wondering how on earth she'd let him talk her into it. She wondered also if she'd deafened him.

'Yes—sorry, didn't mean to scream,' she said, and heard him chuckle.

'Don't worry. I should have warned you it's a bit steep at first. Look down to your left,' he told her, pointing, and she took a nice, deep, steadying breath and peered out of the side.

It was like patchwork, the pattern of fields and roads and hedges laid out beneath them, and far below she could see their shadow, a little blip travelling slowly across the fields. 'It's almost like looking at a map,' she said, surprised.

'Can you see the house?'

She looked back, and there slightly behind them was the house, and the barn which had concealed this tool of Satan she was fool enough to be in at that precise moment.

'Look at the walled garden to the south of the house,' he said. 'Can you see the marks in the grass?'

It took her a moment to work out which bit was the walled garden, but then she saw it—and something else. The pattern of swirls and lines in the grass, scars of previous plantings now long gone.

'I can see the old knot garden design,' she told him, forgetting the flying for a moment in the thrill of discovery. 'I can almost make out the pattern.'

'I'll go lower,' he said, and that was the end of her sanity.

As if someone had reached up into the sky and seized the end of the left-hand wing, the tiny plane seemed to stand on its wingtip in the sky and swoop recklessly down and round.

She gripped the struts, took a huge deep breath and told herself not to be ridiculous. She wasn't feeling sick. She was fine. She was going to be all right—just as soon as it put its wheels back on the ground and the tiny canopy was opened and she could get out and breathe again—

His voice came over the headphones again, slicing through her fantasy. 'Look now—you can see it quite clearly because the grass seems to grow at different speeds.'

She looked again, anchoring herself to a fixed point to give her confused sense of balance something to hang onto and make sense of. 'Oh, yes,' she said weakly. 'I can see it.'

'It would be nice to be able to copy it exactly. I've got some photos I took earlier this year, but it shows better now.'

The only nice thing Georgia could think of was landing, and fast.

'Seen enough?' he said.

'Yes.'

'Shall we fly over the farm? I can show you the rest of the estate, if you like.'

'Do you mind if I wimp out?' she said, suddenly green at the thought of another unnecessary minute in the craft. 'I confess I'm feeling a bit queasy.'

'Sure. Hang on, I'll get you down now. It's a bit wiggly, but it's quick.'

And he throttled back, pulled the flap lever and the little plane zigged and zagged down out of the sky with gratifying speed.

'Waggle your jaw,' he instructed, and she did, popping her ears as they fell through the air and the ground rushed up to meet them.

Seconds later they were stopped, and he cut the engine, hopped out and opened her canopy, helping her as she scrambled out with more enthusiasm than grace.

'Oh, Lord,' she moaned, and wondered if her legs would ever belong to her again.

'Are you OK?'

She nodded, then wished she hadn't. Any movement of her head seemed to make it worse. 'Sorry. I really don't feel all that good—'

'I'll walk you back to the house. I can put the plane away in a moment.'

His arm came round her, offering firm support, and mentally haranguing herself for being a wimp, she leant on him anyway. It was that or fall down, because her legs seemed to belong to someone else and she wasn't sure if she could make it on her own.

He led her into the kitchen, still deserted, and she sank into a chair and tugged at her collar. It felt tight. It wasn't, but it felt as if it was going to strangle her.

'Are you OK?' he asked, concerned.

'I don't know.'

'Cloakroom?' he offered gently, and she nodded. Her insides were rebelling, and she didn't know what she wanted, except to be cooler and have this whirling in her head stop.

She spent five minutes perched on the edge of the loo with her face pressed against the cool china basin, and two things became clear. One, she wasn't about to chuck after all, and two, she had to lie down.

Now.

She opened the door and found Matt propped against

the wall in the hall, hands jammed in his pockets, a worried look on his face.

'Better?'

She shook her head, and stifled the moan. 'I have to lie down,' she muttered, feeling like the biggest wimp in the world. 'I'll be all right if I can just lie down.'

'Come on.' He tucked his arm firmly round her and led her upstairs, into a bedroom. It was cool, the window wide open, and he pulled the curtains to and rummaged in a drawer.

'Here. Take everything off and put this on, and get into bed and stay there till you feel better. It'll soon wear off. There's a bathroom through that door if you need it. I'll be back in a minute.'

He handed her the T-shirt, wonderfully soft and cool, and then left her.

She didn't have enough fight to argue. Indeed, she felt too ill. She undressed, dropping her clothes where they fell, and pulled on the T-shirt. It drowned her, huge and comforting, and she climbed up into the big bed, crawled under the quilt and laid her head carefully down on the pillow.

His bed, she realised dimly. His sheets, cool and fresh and soft. His pillow, with a trace of last night's after-shave on it. Thank God it wasn't sweet and sickly, but clean and subtle. She closed her eyes, willing herself to breathe nice and slowly and relax, and after a moment the nausea receded.

It didn't go, exactly. It just became less threatening, so that she was able to lie there and absorb the full enormity of what she was doing.

She was in his T-shirt, in his bed, in sheets that carried the lingering scent of his body, making a complete fool of herself because she'd been poleaxed by motion sickness in the bowels of that horrible little mosquito—

She moaned and rolled her face into the pillow, her cheeks burning with humiliation. She ought to get up, to go downstairs and outside and look at the garden, as she was supposed to be doing, instead of lying here breathing in his scent and wishing he was here to hold her until everything settled down again.

Huh! In her dreams. He was probably on the phone to Mrs Brooks complaining that she wasn't fulfilling her part of the auction promise!

Matt was racked with guilt. He hadn't thought to ask her if she was all right with flying, and he'd taken her on a roller-coaster as they'd banked over the house and swooped down to the garden.

And now she was feeling horrendous, and it was his fault. Damn.

He dropped several ice cubes into the glass, topped it up with cold water and went upstairs, tapping softly on the door.

'Georgia?'

He heard her tell him to come in, her voice muffled, and he found her curled on her side in the middle of his bed, those amazing green eyes wide open and huge in her pale face.

'How are you?' he asked softly, ignoring the tug of his hormones at the sight of her there in his bed where he'd dreamt about her so vividly last night.

'A bit better. I feel such a fraud—'

'Don't be silly. It was my fault. I was in such a hurry to show you the knot garden, I just didn't think, I'm sorry. I've brought you some iced water.'

He put it down on the bedside table and brushed her

hair gently back from her face with a hand that wanted to curve around the back of her neck and draw her up to his kiss.

Damn. It was madness. He shoved his hand in his pocket.

'I'll leave you. There's a bellpull there over the bed— it rings in the kitchen. Give it a tug if you need anything.'

'I should be looking at your garden,' she said, agitated.

'Forget the garden,' he growled, still cross with himself. 'I'll come up and see you later.'

And he went out, closing the door softly behind him.

Was he mad with her? He'd seemed angry about something. Oh, well, it was too bad. Hoisting herself up on one elbow she took a sip of the chilled water and sighed with relief. Wonderful. She took another sip, and another, and when nothing untoward seemed to happen, she drained the glass.

Bliss. Now all she wanted was to close her eyes...

She must have slept, because the next thing she knew there was a tap on the door and it opened to reveal Matt, still scowling, but not really at her. She had the oddest feeling he was cross with himself.

'How are you?'

She slid up the bed, tugging the quilt up under her arms like a barrier. She dragged a hand through her hair and gave up with it.

'Better, thanks. I must have slept.'

'Good. Everything settled down?'

She nodded, conscious of a nagging hunger. 'What time is it?'

'Nearly one. Mrs Hodges and the children are getting

lunch. I just wondered if you wanted anything to eat or drink.'

'Something simple,' she said. 'Bread?'

'We've got bread and cheese and salad and fruit— shall I bring you up a selection?'

'I'll come down,' she said, and without thinking, threw off the quilt and shifted towards the edge of the bed. Her bare legs dangled over the side, and the silence in the room was suddenly electric. His eyes raked her, tracking hungrily over the long expanse of skin that disappeared under the hem of the embarrassingly short T-shirt, then came back to meet her startled gaze.

For what seemed like an age neither of them moved, then he cleared his throat and backed towards the door.

'I'll tell Mrs Hodges to expect you,' he said in a voice edged with tension, and the door banged shut behind him.

Georgia stared at the door for an endless moment, then dropped her face into her hands with a sound half-laugh, half-wail. What on earth had she been thinking about? Oh, well, so he'd seen her legs. So what? She wore less on the beach.

She slid slowly off the side of the big, high bed. It was a four-poster, of course. Nothing else would have fitted in the room, with its high ceiling and tall, graceful windows and acres of Persian carpets on gleaming oak boards.

A heavy mahogany linen press, a sort of two-storey cupboard, stood against the far wall, and there was a wonderful old chair by the window. She pulled on her clothes and sat on the chair, looking out over the valley and wondering if it was the sort of place she would have lived in with Brian had he not let the money go to his head.

No, she realised almost instantly. Brian would have hated it. Too old, too quaint, the walls sloping, the ceiling sagging, the window frames slightly crooked to accommodate the openings. He'd wanted brash, ostentatious evidence of his wealth—the penthouse with shiny black leather and chrome and glass, a bar in the corner glittering with cut crystal glasses and the serried ranks of spirit bottles, and the sparkle of endless miles of city lights stretching out into the distance.

Not for him the patina of age, the mellow warmth of ancient brick, the fragrance of a magnificent wisteria draping its panicles of tiny mauve flowers in cheerful profusion around the window's edge, framing the soft countryside. Horses were grazing on the distant hillside, and in the background the hum of bees and the muted sound of a tractor floated on the still, scented air.

'Georgia?'

She hadn't even heard him come it, but he was standing there in the middle of the room, watching her with an odd look on his face.

'It's beautiful here,' she said softly.

'It is. I'm very lucky.' He came closer, his eyes tracking over her face, searching it for something. He hunkered down beside her. 'You look better,' he said after a moment.

She smiled. 'I feel better, thanks. I don't know what came over me.'

'My careless manoeuvring. I didn't think about it, and I'm sorry. I should have done. Now I've put you off.'

She shuddered, still not ready to think about being in the machine. It brought it all back too horribly vividly. 'Don't worry. I wasn't very on to start with,' she said with a laugh.

He smiled, his eyes crinkling and his mouth tipping

into that rueful, asymmetric curve she'd been waiting for. She felt something inside her shift, some barrier shored up against intruders giving under the pressure of his smile.

She smiled back, and his eyes locked with hers. Time seemed to stand still for a moment, and for a breathless instant, she thought he was going to kiss her. Then he straightened, holding out his hand, and drew her to her feet. 'Come on,' he said, oddly gruff, and she followed him downstairs to the kitchen.

'Are you all right?' Lucy asked anxiously as they went in.

'Fine,' she laughed. 'I just felt all dizzy.'

'I get dithy on the roundabout in the playground,' Lucy said sympathetically.

'I don't—I want to fly,' Joe said, looking hopefully from her to Matt.

'No,' she said, as Matt said, 'Sure. Whenever you like.'

She glared at him. 'No,' she repeated. 'I don't think so.'

'Aw, Mum, please?' Joe pleaded. 'It looked such fun. We watched you and waved—did you see us?'

She shook her head, cautiously because of the dizziness. 'No, I'm sorry, I didn't. I was too busy trying not to be ill.'

'Poor Mummy,' Lucy said, scrambling up on her knees and reaching over the big table to pat her hand. 'Were you nearly thick?'

She closed her eyes, still unwilling to remember.

'I think we'd better change the subject, chaps,' Matt put in smoothly. 'Now, what are you planning to do this afternoon?'

'Go in a plane,' Joe said firmly.

'Well, you could go in it, of course, and I can show you how the controls work, but we can't actually fly unless your mother agrees.'

'Which she doesn't,' Georgia reminded him.

'Quite. So, what else?'

'I thought we'd go and have a look in the stream, see if there's any minnows,' Mrs Hodges suggested.

'What'th a minnow?' Lucy asked.

'A tiny fish. Sometimes there are lots of them.'

'And can we catch them?' Joe asked.

'No,' Georgia said, earning herself another black look.

'Not for ever, but you can scoop them out of the water and watch them for a minute, then put them back,' Matt told her. 'They don't mind that.'

'Can we do that?' Lucy asked excitedly.

'Oh, I expect so,' Mrs Hodges said with a smile. Joe just looked mutinous, but Georgia refused to give in. He was too small, too precious to send up in that oversized dragonfly.

'How about having some lunch?' Matt said, to Georgia's relief. She needed to eat. The table was laid, and Matt offered her the basket of freshly sliced bread, three sorts, all gorgeous. She took one to start with, eating it dry and with caution, and then had another and another.

A couple of glasses of chilled water clinking with ice, and she was happy again, everything settling back to normal. Maybe now she could do what she was here for.

'So are you all right with the children for a little while, Mrs Hodges?' Matt asked, as if he could read her mind.

'Oh, yes. You two carry on,' she assured him. 'We're quite happy.'

So Matt took her to the old wood-panelled library lined with glass-fronted bookshelves, and showed her the aerial photographs of the knot garden which he'd taken earlier in the year, photographs which she could study without fear or nausea. In fact, she realised, there had been no need for her to go up at all, and the realisation made her cross.

'I could have looked at these this morning,' she told him with an edge to her voice.

He looked apologetic. 'I know. I'm sorry. I didn't realise it would affect you so badly. Most people love it—you can fly around and spy on all the lovely houses, and pick up ideas. There's a wonderful place near here with a gorgeous knot garden covering about an acre—'

'If you're talking about Birchwood, I worked on the restoration.'

'I don't know what it's called. Big Elizabethan place about two miles away.'

She nodded. 'That's right. And I suppose you feel you want the same?' she said a little acidly.

'No,' he told her with a tiny smile, deflecting her barb easily. 'Far too big. I want Heveling's own design restored, including the middle bit. The rest is easy—totally symmetrical, all four corners identical. It's the middle I can't work out. It doesn't seem complete.'

He pushed the photographs towards her. 'Take a look.'

She did, studying the way the marks of the original box hedging were broken and interrupted here and there. It was almost as if—

'Was it a maze?' she asked thoughtfully.

'What?' He sat up straighter and leant over.

'A maze. Could it have been a maze? They used to do that—perhaps it had a fountain in the centre. There's a mark there.'

They studied the photos closely, then he got to his feet.

'Shall we go outside and have a look?' he suggested.

So they strolled out through the heavy oak side door into the balmy warmth of a mid-April afternoon, and Georgia did what she did best.

She stood still, looking around her, seeing not what was there now but what would have been all those years ago. She could hear the cries of the children, the laughter of the women under the tree at the end, the crunch of gravel underfoot as a couple strolled arm in arm.

She could smell the flowers: old roses and honey-suckle and wallflowers in their season; the herbs, crushed underfoot or brushed by long, full skirts of sprigged muslin; the soft mist of water from the fountain cooling the parched summer air.

'Can you picture it?' he murmured.

'Yes,' she said, looking up at him with laughter in her eyes. 'Oh, yes. It's wonderful—so peaceful and beautiful and soothing—and the only thing in the barn is a horse-drawn carriage!'

He chuckled wryly. *'Touché,'* he murmured. 'So, what do you think? Can you do it?'

'Do it?'

'Yes—if I asked you, could you draw up plans to redesign it? Perhaps you could give me a planting scheme for the centre of the knots, and advise me where to get a suitable fountain. Oh, and then there's the rose garden.'

'Rose garden?' she said weakly, wondering how long he expected her to stay tonight. He'd already inadvertently described about a fortnight's work!

'Yes. Apparently there was a rose garden all around the parterre, against the wall, and at the back behind the low formal area. It would be nice to find the original types of roses that might have been here and replant them—if it's possible. They may not still be available.'

'Many of them are,' she assured him, wondering how to tell him she was going to run out of time before she'd opened the first book. Even if she came back for the whole of tomorrow, they could hardly do more than mark out the basic outline of the knot garden and look up a few roses before she'd have to go and put the children to bed.

'I do realise you're busy,' he said, answering at least one of her questions. 'I know you've got Chelsea coming up in a year's time and lots to do for that, and other contracts on the go, but if you felt you could spare some time—'

'It would take a long time to do it properly,' she found herself saying, without any thought for the consequences. She had no time, for heaven's sake, but her mouth just carried on. 'I'd like to research it—see if I can find any planting schemes or anything. Do you have any old documents in the house? Anything which might relate to the garden? Bills for plants, that sort of thing?'

He nodded thoughtfully. 'There are some old papers. I haven't really looked through them. There's a book, though—old, brownish leather—that's got something about the garden in it. I was going to show it to you.'

All Georgia's antennae stood up on end. 'A brownish book?' she said slowly. Surely not. Had the great Humphery Repton himself worked on this garden?

'Yeah—come back in, I'll show you. It's in the library.'

And he took her back inside, opened a cupboard and pulled out a book, placing it in her hands.

She opened it reverently, then looked up at him, stunned. 'You do know what this is, don't you?'

He shook his head. 'No. I was hoping you might tell me.'

A slow smile curved her lips. Excitement beat at her, and she quite forgot the ghastly episode of the microlight.

'It's a *Red Book*—it's Humphrey Repton's record of the work he did here in 1806. Matt, that's so exciting! It'll tell you everything about that parterre, from start to finish. You don't need me at all, it's all in here, every last plant and plan!'

She handed it to him reluctantly. 'Here. It's very valuable. You ought to take good care of it, so many of them have been destroyed.'

He took it, his eyes fixed on hers, and put it down absently on the table beside him.

'Has anyone ever told you,' he said slowly, 'how beautiful you are when your eyes light up like that?'

Georgia swallowed, and was suddenly full of regret that the book had come to light. Without it, she might have spun out her work here for weeks—months even, with enough sleight of hand.

Now, there was no need for her to stay—except the simple, basic need to be near this man from whom common sense told her she should run as fast as her legs would carry her.

He was rich, he liked playing with big boys' toys, and his smile was altogether too disarming. He was about as safe as his little toy plane—and Georgia had had enough time on an emotional roller-coaster with a rich playboy to know she didn't want to do it all over again.

She looked away. 'Don't, Matt. You're trying to flatter me into it,' she said.

He shook his head. 'No. I don't need to. You want to do it, I know you do. It's just a case of finding the time, if you can, to oversee it. I'd pay you of course and as for flattery, I don't need to flatter you. I'm not telling you anything that isn't the truth.'

For an endless moment she stood there, then swallowing hard, she looked away again, her eyes falling on the book. 'Let's see what he says about the parterre,' she suggested hastily, picking it up and sitting down at the desk. Anything but look into those mesmerising eyes and fall any further for that abundant bad-boy charm...

CHAPTER FOUR

SHE let him talk her into doing the garden, of course, as
he'd known she would. It irritated her that he'd been so
right, but she was itching to read the *Red Book*, to find
out as much as she could about the history of the garden.

Although, of course, Repton's garden wasn't the original garden. Most of the house dated from much earlier,
but the garden they were going to restore was the 'new'
garden, the formal setting for the very much more formal
and newer façade.

And yes, she thought with a smile, it had had a maze
in the middle, the plan clearly outlined in the *Book*, and
in the centre of the maze was a fountain.

'You do realise how hard parterres are to look after?'
she'd warned. 'The box hedges need constant clipping.'

He'd just smiled. 'I know. Look on it as a scheme to
create local employment.'

'Distributing your largesse?' she'd said caustically,
and could have bitten her tongue. It wasn't up to her to
criticise, and if he could afford it, why not? And anyway,
he was paying her, too, to restore it, and she was happy
to let him do that, so why not pay a gardener? It wasn't
up to her to tell him how to spend his money, for
heaven's sake!

He'd looked disappointed in her and changed the subject, so she hadn't been able to apologise to him at the
time, and since then there hadn't really been an appropriate occasion.

At least by Tuesday she'd stopped feeling dizzy and

was able to look real food in the eye again, but there was no way she was going up in his toy again—ever.

Which was a shame, because there was something else she wanted to see, another part of the garden which had been destroyed and turned into another ill-kept lawn, and an aerial view might answer some of her questions. She couldn't bring herself to consider it, though.

She mentioned it to him on Thursday, when she rang to ask about something else.

'I don't suppose you want to take some photos of it?' she suggested.

'What—and fly at the same time? I might crash, and you wouldn't want that on your conscience! Why don't you come with me?'

She suppressed the wave of horror at the thought. 'I'd rather not,' she said drily. 'Anyway, I thought you'd taken some before?'

'I did—I went up with Simon—he's my pilot.'

His pilot? Good grief! He had a *pilot*? And probably a chauffeur, to go with the housekeeper and undoubtedly a whole fleet of under-house-parlour maids and gardeners.

The silence stretched on and on, while her mind whirled. Such wealth! And yet he seemed so nice—

'Georgia?'

Her silence must have conveyed something to him, because he sounded concerned.

'Pilot?' she said weakly.

'He tests the experimental planes and the modifications, and works with the designer in the factory.'

'Factory?' Grief, she was beginning to sound simple!

'Yes—I own a microlight factory. I've had it about three years. It was going under and it seemed a shame, so I bought it.'

Just like that. British Aerospace were struggling, so I bought them out. Well, perhaps not British Aerospace, exactly…

'I didn't realise,' she said lamely.

'No reason why you should. Anyway, that's how I got the photos before.'

'And he can't take you up again?'

'If you're sure I can't talk you into it? I could go really carefully—'

'No!' She took a deep breath and shut her eyes, calming herself so she didn't sound like a hysterical virgin who'd accidentally wandered into the Rugby Club changing rooms. 'No, thanks. I'm sorry. But if you could—I just want to see if the design was ever built, because there's no planting record—it might have been abandoned.'

'I ought to make you go—part of your job description, doing the research,' he teased, and she felt a smile tug her lips. She suddenly had a wave of longing to see him again.

'Ha-ha,' she said drily, and then added, because she couldn't help herself, 'I don't suppose you're there this afternoon, are you? The children are at school until five tonight, so I could have another look at the parterre and perhaps we could look out of the window for the other garden, rather than troubling you with the photos. It seems an awful lot of fuss to put you to when you're busy—'

'Sure.'

'—and there probably isn't anything—what did you say?'

'I said sure. I'm here. I'm not busy. Come on over.'

'Oh.' She felt herself collapse with relief, and won-

dered if she was in much deeper than she'd realised.
'Fine. I'll see you shortly.'

She hung up, suppressed a little squeak of excitement
and caught herself preening in the mirror. Was that a
spot coming? Oh, no, it couldn't be! She peered closer.
It wasn't. Relief.

She looked at her make-up drawer, slammed it shut
and made do with a stroke of lipgloss and a quick rake
of her fingers through her hair. Then she put on sun-
glasses, perched on her head like an Alice band, and
cursed herself for her vanity.

They stayed there, though, holding her hair back out
of the way a little and conveniently to hand just in case
the sun should get too strong. At least it was shining, so
she didn't feel too big a fraud!

Murphy pelted onto the drive as she pulled up and
greeted her like a long-lost friend, and Matt wandered
round the corner after him, a glass of something pink
and interesting in his hand.

'Hi,' he said warmly, and taking her elbow, he kissed
her cheek in greeting and then let her go.

What a shame. She scooped her paperwork out of the
car and smiled at him distractedly. He looked gorgeous—casual in old jeans and a loose checked shirt
which had seen better days, old deck shoes on his feet,
his sleeves rolled up—

Was she drooling? The jeans fitted him so faithfully,
cupping him like a lover—

She coloured and reached back into the car, grabbing
her bag. 'Right, that's everything,' she said brightly,
wondering if he thought she'd lost it completely. 'Where
are we going?'

'Upstairs,' he told her, and her wayward thoughts ran
wild again and nearly choked her. 'I thought if we

looked out of the attic window, you'd be able to see the garden from a bit of height—if you're sure I can't persuade you to go up again?'

He was teasing, she realised, his eyes glinting with mischief. His mouth kicked up in that grin again, and she felt something fall out of the pit of her stomach. Did he have any *idea* how incredibly gorgeous he was? she wondered absently.

'No, you can't persuade me to go up in that instrument of torture, thank you,' she said as primly as she could manage. She didn't feel in the least bit prim. In fact she was shocked at herself, shocked and confused and tingling with anticipation all at once. Frankly, she thought she'd get giddy just going up to the attic, but it was nothing to do with heights and everything to do with following that taut, sexy bottom and those endlessly long powerful legs up the stairs.

They'd picked up drinks from the kitchen, a top-up for him and a fresh glass for her of what turned out to be summer-fruit-flavoured iced tea, and she was juggling the glass and her papers and her roller-coaster emotions all at once. Then they reached the attic, dumped their things down and leant out of the window overlooking the garden.

She hoped he'd put her breathlessness down to the long climb up, but with her shoulder up against his lean, hard chest, his arm behind her propped up on the other side of the window as they leant forwards, he was so close she thought he must be able to hear her heart beating!

It had been bad enough the first evening, dancing with him, but she'd been cross then about the auction. She wasn't cross now, just confused and taken aback by feelings that had been dormant so long she'd forgotten what it was like.

'That's the lawn you're talking about, isn't it?' he said, leaning closer so that his arm brushed against her shoulders, making her even more aware.

'Yes—yes, that's the one, I think.' Oh, Lord, did she sound as vacant as she thought she did? His other arm, the one that wasn't behind her, was pointing out various features in the garden, and she should have been riveted.

She was, but not by his words or the things he was pointing out! It was his hand, instead, that tantalised her, strong straight fingers, a firm wrist leading to a solid, well-muscled forearm. His cuffs were turned back a couple of times, and she could see a scatter of soft brown hair peeping out from under the end of the sleeve.

His hand was brown, weatherbeaten and interesting, with little scars here and there. It was a real hand, not a city hand but a hand that knew real work, a strong hand—a very male hand. She had a sudden need to feel it against her skin, to have him lift it and lay it against her throat in the open neck of her blouse—

'What do you think?'

She blinked. 'Think?'

'About the statue.' He straightened and looked down at her, so close she could feel the soft puff of his breath as he spoke. 'You weren't listening,' he chastised gently.

She shook her head and dredged up a smile. 'I'm sorry. I was miles away, thinking about something else. What did you say about the statue?'

'I wondered if there was any record of it, and where it was meant to be. There are various bits of statuary around the place. I suspect my uncle just had no idea how valuable they were or he would have sold them, too. This one's a damsel draped fetchingly in a scrap of gauze. I call her Aphrodite, because she's so lovely.'

His voice trailed off, his eyes fixed on hers. Something happened in their strange ice-blue depths, something elemental that found an answering chord in the wild beating of her heart.

He's going to kiss me, she thought, and then she stopped thinking because his hand came up, the one she'd been fantasising about, and as if he'd read her mind he touched it lightly against the soft, warm skin of her throat and held it there.

'Your heart's pounding,' he murmured, and his thumb grazed idly against the leaping pulse.

She thought her knees would give way, just looking into his eyes and seeing the pupils flare and darken. He's looking at me like that, she thought in wonder. Me! And then he slid his hand round the back of her neck, threading his fingers through her hair and drawing her closer as his head came down and his mouth brushed lightly against hers.

A tiny moan escaped her, and he murmured her name against her lips. The soft haze of his breath teased her skin, and she sagged against him, her legs as weak as knotted cotton. He caught her with his other arm, his hand splayed firmly against the small of her back, holding her against him so she could feel the rise and fall of his chest, the firm columns of his legs, the hard and insistent pressure of a very masculine response.

'Georgia,' he said again, and then his mouth angled over hers and he deepened the kiss.

Heat raced through her like wildfire, melting her resistance, sweeping aside all her sensible notions about propriety and abstinence and independent thinking. She was putty in his hands, and like a master sculptor he moulded her to his body and held her mouth until she could have wept with need.

Finally, when she thought she'd die of frustration and lack of air, he lifted his head, tucking her under his chin and holding her against his chest so that her ear was against the thudding of his heart and she could feel the ragged rise and fall of his chest beneath her cheek.

'Matt?' she whispered.

'Shh. Give me a minute,' he said gruffly, and his hands moved lightly over her back, absently stroking her, gentling her like a groom with an injured horse.

Gradually their breathing steadied, and he straightened up and looked down at her, giving her a crooked little smile. 'OK?' he said softly.

She nodded numbly, still shocked by the force of her response. 'I think so,' she said, testing the strength of her legs and finding them wanting. She leant against the side of the dormer window, taking strength from the solid structure of the building. It had been there a couple of hundred years. It could hold her up for a few minutes!

'I've been wanting to do that since Friday,' he confessed, his voice oddly taut, and she realised that far from being over, the kiss had barely started, the first tentative notes of a symphony, and their bodies, like the orchestra, were simply tuning up ready for the performance.

She looked away, down into the garden. Funny, it hadn't changed in the last couple of minutes, and yet she felt it should look different. There should be a bomb crater in the middle of it, or something equally momentous, she thought—something to mark the change in their relationship.

'I don't do things like this,' she said, her voice breathy

and distracted. She tried again. 'I'm a mother—a single
parent. I have to set an example.'

'Does that mean you don't have a right to a life of
your own?' he asked softly.

A light breeze from the window cooled her skin, taking out the heat his kiss had put in her cheeks. She
shivered, hugging herself, and he pulled the window shut
and turned her so she was facing him. 'Georgia? What
is it?'

She shook her head, not sure herself what was wrong.
Her body wanted him, but her mind, now it was coming
back into her possession, was screaming in panic.

'Please—I don't like feeling like this—'

'Like what? Aroused?'

Heat scorched her cheeks again. 'Out of control,' she
corrected. 'You and me, up here all alone, with nothing
to disturb us but the cobwebs. It frightens me.' Why had
she said that? She wasn't frightened—was she? And she
realised she was. She was terrified.

His hand came up and cupped her cheek, a tender
gesture that made her want to lean into his hand and cry
with frustration. 'Don't be frightened. I'd never hurt
you,' he murmured.

'I didn't mean that.' She struggled to explain, and
couldn't. She didn't understand it herself. 'I've spent
years getting my life together, since Brian died. I'd finally done it—and now I feel threatened, and I don't
like it.'

'Brian?' he said, his face creasing in a frown. 'Brian
Beckett—of course. That's where I know you from.'

She looked up at him, startled, and watched as recollection dawned on his face. Recollection and anger.
'You were pregnant. He'd invited a whole crowd of us
back without warning, and you were lying down resting.

The baby—Joe, I suppose—was asleep, and you had to get up and wait on us. He criticised you because you didn't have enough of the right sort of nibbles and things in the house, and the tonic water wasn't cold enough.'

She remembered—remembered Brian's anger, the feel of his hand against her cheek—and the kind touch of a stranger, a gentle man who'd laid his hand on her shoulder and offered silent support.

Matthew. Matthew Fraser. Of course. That was where she'd heard the name, years ago.

'You must be a financial something,' she said, and felt the momentous desire drain away, leaving her cold and shaken. She thought she'd got away from that world, from the lying and cheating and backstabbing. Yet here she was, sucked back into it by a playboy with nothing else to do but toy with her.

'I was,' he told her. 'I was an investment analyst. Then my uncle died and left me this pile of rubble and weeds, and I sold my portfolio and poured everything into it, I supposed that makes me a farmer now—not forgetting a microlight manufacturer!' he said with a grin, but unusually the grin failed to reach her.

All she could think about was Brian, and the fact that this man moved in the same circles.

She'd never forget the way Brian had lashed out at her because the tonic wasn't cold.

Then later, when everyone had gone, he'd drunk himself into a stupor and she had slept with Joe, praying that Brian would leave her alone. It had been the beginning of a nightmare that had ended in his death, and now Matt had reminded her of it and it had all come flooding back.

Not again, she thought. Not another man from that world.

Not any man, in fact. Not after all that had happened.

'Georgia?'

She couldn't look at him, didn't want him to see the emotions she knew would be revealed on her face.

'I'm all right,' she said, her voice sounding distant and a little chilling. She moved away from the window, her hands cupping her arms and hugging them, holding herself together. 'Um—we were going to look at the parterre.'

'We need to talk,' he said gently.

'No. There's nothing to say, Matt. I'll do your garden, but that's all. I can't afford to get emotionally involved with you, and I certainly don't intend to sleep with you without being emotionally involved—'

'Have I asked you to?'

She shook her head. 'Not in so many words, but your body was pretty easy to read.'

'So was yours.'

There was no answer to that—no convincing answer, anyway. She shuffled her papers restlessly, picked up her drink, sipped it, put it down.

'Matt—'

'Georgia—'

They spoke together, and he smiled crookedly. 'I was going to apologise. Not for kissing you, because I don't regret it for a moment, but for making you feel uncomfortable. I didn't mean to do that.'

She didn't regret the kiss, either—just the fact of who he'd been, who he was. She wouldn't have minded if he'd been a hired hand, an ordinary man who got up in the morning and went to work and came home—

'Come round the farm with me. I have to go over to the other end of the estate to pick up some stuff from the estate office. Come with me—we'll take the Discovery and go round the fields instead of on the road. It'll help you get a feel for the place.'

She wanted to argue, but he was right, of course. She did need a feel for it if she was to play a part in its restoration—and anyway, whatever her mouth was saying, the rest of her disagreed. She wanted to be near him, to spend the rest of the afternoon in his company.

'No more kisses?' she challenged, and he smiled, a cock-eyed smile that softened the strain in his eyes and made her forget who he was.

'No more kisses,' he said, and his voice was full of teasing regret.

'OK,' she found herself saying, and wondered if she was quite mad, or if it was Matt's job to finish sending her round the bend!

She was so lovely. He sneaked a sideways glance at her as they bounced around the edge of a field, and couldn't quite believe his luck.

Not that it was all plain sailing.

Clearly she was haunted by the memory of Brian Beckett, the bastard who'd married her and then proceeded to shred her self-esteem.

Had he hit her? His fists tightened on the steering wheel, and he had a moment of intense and un-Christian gratitude that the man was dead. He'd been a thoroughly pompous idiot, stuffed up with his own importance, and desperate to show off his wealth.

Matt hated that. The City did it to some people, turned them from perfectly nice, ordinary men into raving megalomaniacs. He couldn't imagine that Brian would have been that awful at first, or Georgia wouldn't surely have married him? She struck him as very decisive, knowing what she wanted and, more's the pity, what she didn't want.

Just now he seemed to be top of that particular list.

'Is that flax?' she asked, pointing across the valley to a field tinged with blue.

He dragged his attention back to what he was supposed to be doing. 'Yes. It's just beginning to flower. It's lovely, isn't it?' Not as lovely as you, though. Oh, damn.

He forced himself to concentrate, pointing things out to her—a line of ancient oaks that marked the original road to the farm, the site on the hillside of the windmill that had ground all the flour for the estate, the wood still full of deer that grazed on the wheat and drove the farm manager crazy.

They pulled up on a rise, looking back over the house, and he told her a little of the history of the estate.

And as he talked, telling her about his property, he realised just how much he'd come to love it, and why it was so important to him. He remembered it from years ago, before his uncle's drinking and gambling had deprived the estate of its income and management and let it go to rack and ruin.

It had been beautiful then, and it would be beautiful once more. Matt looked around, at the land and buildings that he was fortunate enough to call his own, and vowed that he would do it all justice.

'You love it, don't you?' she said softly, and he nodded.

'Yes. Yes, I do.'

A fierce pride gripped him, and he struggled to explain it to Georgia.

'I'm just a caretaker,' he said simply. 'A custodian. It's mine to enjoy for my lifetime, but I'm just one link in the chain. I have no right to change it or damage it—just to look after it, to take it on into the next generation.'

He shot her a smile. 'It's a great privilege—and an awesome responsibility. Sometimes it scares me spitless. At other times, like when we're planning the knot garden, it makes me humble to think that I've got a chance to give something back, to say thank you, in a way, to the house for all the pleasure and beauty it's brought into my life.'

He fell silent, wondering if she understood or if she thought he was mad. She'd been married to Brian Beckett—for all he knew, she liked the monied life and would find his attitude bizarre.

He started the engine again and threw the car into gear, bumping down the hill to the estate yard and turning in front of the office. Whatever, she'd made it clear she didn't want to take their personal relationship any further, and he'd have to respect that, like it or not.

Just then, he didn't like it at all!

CHAPTER FIVE

'PLEATHE, Mummy, *pleathe*!'

'No, darling, we can't. He doesn't want us there.'

'But Mithith Hodgeth makth the betht chocolate cake—'

'No, Lucy.'

'But he said he'd let me taxi the plane—'

'*No*, Joe!' She took a deep breath, and started again. 'We can't keep pestering him. He doesn't want us all there every weekend. We could have a picnic—'

'But we weren't there at all last weekend, or the one before. It's been *weeks*.'

Joe was right. It was three weeks since they'd all been there, and over two since the day he'd kissed her. She hadn't been back since, and to tell the truth she could do with a day there to look at the garden again and survey it accurately.

She'd done lots of research on paper, but it wasn't the same as standing there, breathing in the scent of it, touching it, feeling it.

She felt the same about Matt, but like the secret garden of the story, it was one door she wanted to keep firmly shut and locked. She didn't want to be close enough to smell him, touch him, feel him.

Liar, her alter ego taunted her, and she closed her eyes and tried very, very hard not to think about the feel of his body against hers. She tried not to remember the dreams, wild and vivid and definitely X-rated, with the orchestra well into the symphony and running down to the final chords—

'He's here! Mum, he's here!'

She opened her eyes, stunned, and as if her fevered imagination had conjured him out of thin air, she saw Matt striding purposefully up the drive, hands jammed into the pockets of those jeans that knew his body so well. His car—the Discovery today—was hitched up on the kerb, and he looked lean and fit and too good to be true.

Her body screamed with recognition, and she gave it a mental slap and went to open the door.

'Hi,' she said, conscious of the smile that stretched her mouth almost to her ears.

'Hi, yourself.' He bent and dropped the lightest of kisses on her mouth, and she went up in flames.

'Um—what are you doing here?' she asked, horribly aware of the children's insatiable curiosity and their enthusiasm for Matt and his house.

'I was passing.' He smiled, that crinkly, lopsided smile that did her in, and looked past her. 'Hi, kids. Busy today?'

Uh-oh. 'We wanted to come and see you,' Joe said with customary bluntness, 'but Mum said you wouldn't want us.'

'Well, she's wrong. Actually I came to ask if you'd like to come round for a barbecue—it's a gorgeous day, and I thought it might be rather fun.'

'Mum said we'd have a picnic, but I don't suppose there's any food. There never is,' Joe told him without any respect for Georgia's feelings.

'I've been busy,' she began weakly.

'We've got lots of food. Mrs Hodges doesn't have

anything else to worry about, so there's always tons to eat, so we could have a picnic instead, if you wanted.'

'By the river?'

'Could we catch the minnowth?'

'Can Murphy come too?'

She wavered, torn between accepting so she could look at the garden—and coincidentally Matt!—and refusing and ruining the children's evident happiness. In the end, of course, it wasn't really her choice at all, and she crumpled under their combined pressure.

Not that it took a lot to convince her, if she was honest. Just standing in the same room as him made her realise how much more alive she felt now than she had in the previous two weeks.

'All right,' she conceded, and the children whooped with delight and pelted upstairs to find shoes and socks and grab jumpers, just in case it got cold.

'That was low and sneaky,' she told him, trying to keep the smile off her face, and he grinned, quite unrepentant.

'Not very. Anyway, you haven't been over for ages. I wondered if you'd had time to think any more about the garden.'

She'd hardly thought about anything else, but she wasn't going to tell him that! He was wrecking her livelihood, between planning his garden during the day when she should have been working on other projects, and interfering with her sleep at night.

The children crashed back down into the hall before she could answer, and she picked up her work on his garden, and a cardigan, and looked up at him. 'I'll follow you.'

'I want to go in the Discovery!' Joe said instantly.

'Thoe do I!' Lucy chipped in.

'No, you can come with me.'

'I can take them.'

'They need booster seats. They have to go in the back—they're under twelve. It's a lot of trouble.'

'Why don't you all come, and I can drive you home later? That way you can have a glass of wine with your lunch and relax.'

'And you can't.'

He smiled. 'I'll live. Come on, it's only five minutes down the road.'

And that was it. They piled their bits and pieces into the back of his car, took the booster seats out of hers and put them on the back seat, and off they went.

The children squeaked and bounced nearly all the way, because they could see so much more out of the high vehicle than out of the car. If it hadn't been beneath her dignity, Georgia would have squeaked and bounced all the way as well, because sitting next to Matt and listening to the mellow rumble of his voice as she watched him out of the corner of her eye was doing extraordinary things to her blood pressure.

In fact her dignity was hanging by a thread, and when he told a dreadful joke she laughed till her sides ached, just to let out the tension.

Oh, darn the man! He was too gorgeous. It wasn't fair. How was she supposed to remain indifferent to him when he was so funny and human and just downright sexy?

Murphy greeted them, thumping his tail against the side of the car and washing the children with huge swipes of that wonderful pink tongue. Lucy shrieked and giggled, and Joe pulled a face, but Murphy was unrepentant. He climbed into the back of the car and ran about all over her drawings, and when Matt chased him out he ran off up the drive after Scally, looking for all the world like a greyhound in a wig.

'Wow, he can move!' Georgia said, astonished.

'Oh, yes. He's as fit as a flea. Poor old Scally gets given the run-around several times a day, but they love each other really.'

Scally had shot up the side of the barn and was perched on the ledge above the door, giving Murphy the evil eye. He didn't look as if he loved the dog at all, but Murphy didn't care. He'd found something smelly in the grass and was rolling in it with huge enthusiasm.

'You're disgusting,' Matt told him affectionately, and led them all into the kitchen through the back door.

Mrs Hodges was up to her elbows in washing up, and greeted them cheerily. Within seconds both children had teatowels and were drying up, and without any of the ill humour to which Georgia was normally treated.

Amazing. They were discussing the contents of the picnic, and what they would like to eat, and Matt jerked his head towards the door and led her outside again.

'Let's go and look at the garden. There are roses coming out round the edge—I thought you might be able to tell me what they are—and I want your opinion on something else.'

They crunched round the side of the house on the gravel path, and opened the door into the walled garden. There was a gazebo there, a little brick summer house with a pointed octagonal roof, and he led her over to it and opened the sagging door.

'I wanted to restore this. What do you think?'

She stepped inside and looked around, enchanted by the delightful little room. The windows were broken, the floor was strewn with old leaves and the ceiling festooned with cobwebs, but it was lovely.

'Oh, yes,' she said softly. 'It's—'

'Romantic?' His voice was low and soft and slightly husky. 'Can't you just imagine a beautiful girl in a long, flowing skirt blushing prettily while her beau presented her with roses? And maybe he'd even steal a kiss...'

She suddenly realised that they were all alone, and her heart kicked against her ribs. Their eyes locked, and without a word he drew her into his arms and lowered his mouth to hers.

She hadn't realised how much she'd longed for him until he touched her. Her palms flattened against his chest to push him away, but lay quiet instead, feeling the pounding of his heart and the warmth of his body seeping through his shirt.

His lips left hers, trailing a line of hot, open-mouthed kisses over the angle of her jaw and down her throat, into the hollow where her heart beat a wild tattoo.

'I thought we weren't going to do this,' she protested feebly, fingers curling into his shirt to hold him closer.

He chuckled, his breath puffing against her throat, and lifted his head. His eyes were creased with humour.

'Want me to stop?'

No, she didn't. She closed her eyes, unable to fight him, and his mouth brushed hers again and again. 'Unfair,' she whispered, and he laughed softly and kissed her again, then let her go.

The wave of disappointment stunned her, until she saw his eyes again. Dark with desire, his face naked with longing, it was quite clear he would have been happy to carry on.

And yet he'd stopped, because he knew she wanted him to.

'Come on,' he said softly. 'We'll go and walk round the garden and look at the roses and try to stop thinking about it. Maybe then I won't disgrace myself with you in front of Mrs Hodges and the children.'

Georgia was very afraid she was going to disgrace herself without any help from him, but she didn't say so. Instead they went back out into the glorious sunshine and strolled along the edge of the old rose border, while she peered at one tangled mess after another and tried to pretend she was interested Which she would have been, of course, at any other time or with any other man!

'They need a lot of work,' she said thoughtfully, finally distracted by the plants. 'Some of them would be better pulled out, but it would help if we knew what was coming out so we could replace it.'

'Doesn't the book have planting plans?' he said.

'No. Not for this bit. Repton just suggested roses and left it at that, so really you could put in anything you liked that was an old rose.'

'I took some photos last summer when they were in flower—would that help, or do you just want to wait until they come into flower again this year? It shouldn't be long.'

She looked at the roses, the buds fat and ready to burst open on several of them, and shook her head. 'I'll wait. The real thing tells you so much more—sometimes the scent is important.'

She turned, and found he'd moved closer to see what she was looking at. So much closer, in fact, that her hands came up to stop her bumping into him and landed softly on his chest.

He smiled, just a faint twist of his lips, and moved away. 'We'd better not start that again,' he murmured, in the nick of time, because the gate in the wall opened and the children came running in with Murphy.

'Mrs Hodges says lunch is ready when we are, she's

put in mineral water and do you want a bottle of wine
as well?' Joe said breathlessly, skidding to a halt at their
feet.

'Not for me,' Georgia said.

'Mineral water will be fine. We'll be there in a minute.'

They ran off, the dog bounding beside them, delighted
with young and energetic company, and Matt turned to
her. 'Shall we come back and do this later? How much
time have you got?'

All the time in the world for you, she wanted to say,
but her body and her common sense were at odds again,
and anyway, her conscience was playing up. She had
other clients to deal with, other work to do.

'I ought to finish a design for my London client this
weekend—we've done most of the work, but I've left
my team pretty much alone with it and I ought to have
a look and see what they've done—make sure it's all
right. He's a bit of a pain, the client.'

'Team?' Matt said curiously. 'I thought you worked
alone.'

She laughed. 'Alone? Good heavens, no. There are
four of us. I've got two draughtsmen, a visualiser and
me—I'm the plant person, really, and the designer. I
couldn't possibly do all I do on my own.'

He looked a trifle stunned, as if he hadn't realised the
scale of her operation. 'I ought to show you the studio
one day—it's in the garage. We converted it, but left the
door, because the planners didn't want it looking different. I'll show you later when you take us back, if you
like.'

'Thanks.'

They headed back towards the kitchen, Matt in a
thoughtful silence, and Georgia looked around her.
Beyond the formal gardens and the cluster of farm build-

ings at the back was open parkland on three sides, studded with magnificent trees and little woods and crisscrossed with paths and bridleways, beyond which lay the farm.

In the distance, up by a wood, she could see deer grazing watchfully on the fringes of the parkland, and someone riding along one of the tracks. It looked peaceful and bucolic and gloriously English.

What was it like, she wondered, to be part of this? To own it, to be the caretaker and custodian, as Matt saw himself?

An awesome responsibility, and a tremendous privilege.

A little shiver ran over her, and she hugged herself, despite the warmth of the day.

'Cold?' he asked, and she shook her head.

'Someone walked over my grave,' she said, and laughed awkwardly. 'Silly expression.'

His arm came round her briefly, warm and solid and comforting, and she felt a pang of regret when he removed it and ushered her through the kitchen door and back to the others.

The children were sparkling and laughing, and Mrs Hodges was still unbelievably putting things into the hamper.

'Good grief, we won't need to eat again for weeks,' Georgia said with a surprised laugh, eyeing the bulging contents.

'That's it now. I just thought I'd give you plenty of choice, and I know Murphy will eat anything you don't manage.'

Murphy was sitting, his face on a level with the hamper, showing his enthusiasm for its contents. 'Later,' Matt told him, and hoisted the hamper into his arms.

'Right, we'll be down by the river, Mrs H, if anyone needs me.'

'Righty-ho. Have a nice time.' And she ruffled the children's hair affectionately as they skidded past and rushed out to the car, Murphy in hot pursuit.

They bumped and meandered their way down to the riverbank, sending the deer fleeing for cover. Murphy wasn't in the car, but ran alongside, his long grey form stretched out in evident enjoyment as he ate up the ground.

Matt parked in the shade of a big alder tree and opened the tailgate. 'Right, everybody, come and help.'

He gave Lucy and Joe two blankets to spread out, Georgia a couple of cushions, and hefted the hamper into his arms. 'Let's see what she's packed, shall we?' he said with a grin, and headed for a little sunny spot in amongst the trees.

The river was more of a stream, bubbling and gurgling over a broken branch that had fallen in and dammed it slightly. It was restful and beautiful, and the food was superb. They ate chicken legs and pâté and fresh crusty rolls and salads, all washed down with ice-cold sparkling mineral water, and followed by fresh fruit and great slabs of fruit cake and cheese, and Georgia wondered if she'd ever had a more perfect day in her life.

The children, full to the brim, were paddling in the stream, catching minnows with little nets and putting them in jam jars to watch them for a minute before putting them back.

Murphy was making the most of a couple of boned chicken legs, three rolls and an apple core, and having scavenged until he was sure there was nothing left, he flopped down beside them with a huge sigh and went to sleep.

Which left Matt and Georgia together, lying on the blankets with their heads together on the cushions, face to face, eyes locked. He had beautiful eyes, she thought dreamily. Long lashes, clear whites, that interesting icy blue outlined in navy—fascinating.

His nose was a little crooked, and she wondered if it had been broken at some point. And then, of course, there was his mouth—firm lips, not too full, the skin around them shadowed faintly with stubble, not smiling for once.

Her eyes flicked back to his, taking in the darkening pupils, the soft expression, the carefully banked desire, and her breath caught.

'You're beautiful,' he murmured, and a blunt fingertip traced the outline of her lips. 'I want to kiss you.'

A tiny moan escaped her, and he chuckled. 'Hell, isn't it? We ought to just give in.'

She rolled onto her back. 'No. I can't. I have to keep my life on track, and you keep doing this to me—tantalising me with glimpses of what I can't have—'

'Yes, you can.'

'No, I can't. I have to be independent.'

'I haven't asked you to marry me and give up your job and be my love slave,' he said drily.

Part of her panicked at the thought. A larger, more sensible part knew that he wasn't like Brian, and that in itself was dangerous. Stolen kisses and romantic picnics in the soft, sweet grass were just the thin end of the wedge, and she knew that she would yield ultimately, not just her body but her soul.

And then what? He'd made it pretty clear just then he didn't want any more than just her body!

She sat up, putting some distance between them.

'What are the children doing?' she said in a strained voice.

'Playing in the river. You can hear them. They're fine. Stop changing the subject.'

He drew her down onto the rug again, and kissed her, just lightly, just once, and she felt herself melt and weaken and surrender.

'What are you doing tonight?'

'Working,' she said, her voice vague and elsewhere.

'I want to take you out to dinner.'

'No.'

'You say that a lot. Why can't you just say yes?'

His lips were smiling, but his eyes were serious, and she knew she was getting in too deep. She sat up again and called the children.

'Come on, we have to go. I've got work to do.'

'You need to survey the garden.'

'I do. I'll come over with Terry next week, if that's all right. You don't need to be here, just so long as we can get into the garden. Joe, Lucy, now, please!'

She stood up and packed things haphazardly into the picnic hamper, until Matt took them out of her hands and redid it himself. The children came grumbling and whingeing, but she was insistent, and within minutes they were headed back.

They dropped off the picnic things and Murphy, and Matt drove them back to their house in a tense silence. The children were quiet, tired after their busy time in the river, and Georgia was wishing she hadn't offered to show Matt the studio.

She just wanted him to go, to leave her alone for a while. He was too disturbing, too interesting, too persuasive for her peace of mind.

She needn't have worried. He dropped them off,

waved them goodbye and drove off without a backwards glance. So much for her worries. Obviously putting him off enough times had done exactly that—put him off.

And this disappointment was too perverse for words!

She put the kettle on, made a cup of tea and went into the studio to work, leaving the children stretched out in front of the television.

Time blurred. She worked until she had finished the London job, pulling together the work her team had done, and then sat back, satisfied, and glanced at her watch.

Good heavens, she thought. It's six o'clock!

She put the finished project on the top of the drawing board by the door, filed the other drawings in the plan chest and looked around.

That was better. Tidier, and ready for the next project—a detailed survey and planting plan of Matt's garden, with visuals.

Humming to herself, she went through into the house, just as Joe came flying down the stairs, eyes wide.

'Mum, help, it's on fire!' he cried.

'What?' Fear running cold down her spine, she looked up and saw flames flickering in his bedroom. 'Dear God—where's Lucy?'

'In the sitting room watching telly.'

'Go outside, quickly. Tell Jenny to call the fire brigade. Whatever you do, don't come back in!'

She pushed him through the door, ran for the sitting room and grabbed Lucy, and in a moment of lunacy snatched up the baby photos and childhood albums from the bookcase.

'Out,' she said, pushing Lucy through the door as the fire caught hold and spread to the landing.

Her neighbours were gathering on the drive and she

ran to them, checking on Joe, then turning back to watch as her house, their home, went up in flames.

'The *Red Book*,' she said, suddenly cold, and ran back.

'Georgia, no!' Jenny screamed, but she ignored her. She knew where it was—in the studio, near the door, just next to the finished London project. Anyway, the fire was only upstairs, she'd be safe.

She ran through the hall to the studio, grabbed Repton's *Red Book of Heveling Hall*, and the London project, and shot out again just as the house seemed to explode with rage.

Flaming curtains flapped through the open windows, and they could hear the roar of the flames as the fire caught hold and spread. Then in the distance they heard the fire engines.

'Come on, out of the way,' Jenny was saying, and marshalled them all off the drive and over into her garden as the appliances screamed up to the house and the firemen started to run towards it, unreeling hoses.

'Anyone inside?' a man yelled. 'Any pets?'

'No. All out,' a neighbour confirmed, and suddenly Georgia couldn't look any more. She turned her face away, hugging the children against her, the book and the project still in her hands.

'It's my fault,' Joe was saying, but she shushed him.

'It's all right. You saved us. Don't worry now.'

What had he meant? Had he started the fire?

A shudder ran through her. She couldn't cope with this. Not again, not another new start, with everything gone. Jenny took the books from her hands and put them in her house, then came back.

'Are you all right?' she asked anxiously.

No, I want Matt, she thought, and then as if by magic

he was there, pushing his way through the crowd, drawing her and the children into his arms.

'Thank God you're safe,' he said hoarsely, and she dropped her head onto his chest and burst into tears. He held her, murmuring comforting words as the smoke and flames hissed and spat just behind them.

It took only a few minutes to subdue the flames and get the fire under control, and then the firemen started opening windows and ventilating the house. The smell was awful, acrid and bitter and clinging.

'I want to see.'

'Don't be silly. You can't go in there. It's not safe.'

'I want to know how bad it is,' she insisted.

'Stay here.' He went towards the house, had a brief conversation with one of the fire officers and came back towards them with the man.

'Mrs Beckett? I'm the chief fire officer—Bernie Warren. Sorry about the house, but at least you're all safe and it's all under control now.'

'Can I go in?'

He shook his head. 'Not yet, I'm sorry. We need to get the roof off and make sure the rafters aren't smouldering,' he explained. 'It's a bit of a mess, but the only fire damage is in the bedrooms. Any idea how it could have started?'

She looked at Joe, clinging to her, eyes wide with shock. 'I'm not sure. Joe, what happened, darling?' she asked, sliding her arm round his shoulders and hugging him firmly. 'Can you tell us?'

'It was the paper,' he mumbled. 'I put in on top of the lamp, and it went all crinkly and brown and funny. I've done it before. I never thought it would catch fire—'

'Just that? Just one piece of paper?'

He nodded. 'But I put it in the wastepaper basket, and

all the paper caught fire and then the curtain caught fire and I tried to put it out with water from the bathroom but it was too big, and I didn't know what to do—'

He started to cry, his shoulders heaving, his body trembling with shock, and she hugged him hard. 'It's all right. It was an accident. It's all right, Joe. It's all right.'

'Well, that sounds pretty conclusive,' the fire officer said. 'I'll write my report on that basis—it's backed up by everything we've seen inside. Now, the thing is, madam, you aren't going to be able to stay here tonight. Is there anything you'd like us to bring out for you? I'm afraid all the clothes upstairs will have been smoke damaged if not burnt, so they won't be any use until they've been washed, but is there anything else?'

She shook her head. 'No. Nothing—unless there's anything in the tumble drier in the kitchen.'

'I'll get someone to have a look. What about keys to the property, handbag, money, that sort of thing?'

She nodded, trying to think. 'There's a bag in the hall—or it might be in the kitchen. A big black leather bag full of all sorts of things. I can't go anywhere without that.'

'Right. I'll get it sorted out for you. What about valuables? Paintings, furniture, a collection of any sort?'

She shook her head. 'No valuables. Only the children.' Her voice caught, and he gave her a sympathetic smile.

'Bit of a shock when this sort of thing happens, but we've done what we can to minimise the damage. It's mostly smoke that's the problem. We're just cutting out the floor and ceiling and making sure there aren't any hot spots left—we don't want the fire catching hold again once we leave. We've got to take the roof off over that end for the same reason, but we'll cover it with a tarpaulin so it's weather-tight. You don't want any more damage.'

'No. Thank you.'

The man nodded. 'OK. Well, you can't go in there tonight, obviously. We'll carry on now, but you should be able to get in tomorrow and salvage your possessions, I expect. I should go and have a good night's rest. Are you all right for accommodation tonight?'

She stared blankly at the man. She hadn't even thought about it.

'I'll find a hotel, I suppose,' she said numbly.

'They'll stay with me. Here.' Matt gave the fire officer a card from his breast pocket. 'Perhaps you could ring if there's a problem.'

And without waiting for any further discussion, Matt collected the bag and keys from the fire officer who brought them out, put Georgia and the children in the car and took them back to Heveling.

'But I ought to be there,' she protested, watching over her shoulder as the firemen started tackling the roof.

'No. We'll take the children home, then I'll bring you back if you want, but I don't think they need to be here any longer.'

He was right, of course. They looked shattered, their eyes red-rimmed and shocked, their faces pinched and drawn.

'Mrs H will look after them—bath them and give them supper and put them to bed. She's good with them, and they like her.'

And me? she thought. Who's going to bath me and give me supper and put me to bed?

She had a sudden, desperate longing to feel his arms around her again, holding her close against his chest and

comforting her. She rested her head back against the
head restraint and let out a ragged sigh.

'Are you all right?'

'Not really. My home's just gone up in flames, my
workplace is trashed, everything's either burnt or
soaked, and I don't know what's going to happen to
us—'

She stopped, biting her lip to hold down the hysteria,
and he reached out a comforting hand and rested it on
her thigh.

'It'll be all right.'

'I got the Red Book out,' she told him, and flinched
when he glared at her.

'You what! You went back in?'

'I had to. It was quite safe—'

'You idiot! You could have been killed!'

She bit her lips and stifled the tears. 'No. There was
no risk. Please, Matt, don't shout at me.'

'I'm sorry.'

His hand, big and warm and firm, squeezed her leg.
She felt lost when he took it away and returned it to the
steering wheel to swing onto the drive.

'We're home,' he said, and she wanted to weep, because it wasn't home, and it couldn't be, and she didn't
have one any longer.

'Come on, kids,' he said gently, and led them into the
kitchen. He picked up the phone, spoke briefly and seconds later Mrs Hodges bustled in, her face creased with
worry.

'Oh, my poor lambs,' she said, and engulfed the children with her kindness. Then she looked up, caught
Georgia's eye and turned to Matt.

'Take Mrs Beckett into the drawing room and give

her a drink, Matt. She looks as if she could do with it. I'll look after the children.'

On autopilot, she followed him, down the hall to the drawing room with its big old furniture and comfy sofas. Murphy came too, his nails clattering on the polished boards, and Matt closed the door with a little click.

'Whisky or brandy?' he asked, but she shook her head.

'Just hold me,' she pleaded, and as his arms came round her, her bravado ran out and the tears streamed down her cheeks.

'Don't worry, you're all safe, that's all that matters,' he said softly, but it wasn't all.

'I got the photos out—the baby photos of the children, and their school photos, things like that—but there were so many things upstairs—little treasures, things they've made me that I was going to keep for ever—'

And with a hiccuping sob, she gave in to the luxury of being held by him, and burrowed into his arms. He scooped her up and sat down with her on his lap, and she curled up against his shoulder like a cat. She felt shaken and bereft and helpless. She'd lost everything, or almost everything, but Matt was there, holding her, taking care of her.

One thing nagged at her, though. 'How come you were there? Did Jenny ring you?' she asked.

He gave a short huff of laughter that lifted his chest under her hand. 'No. I was coming to see you. I thought I'd talk you into letting me get a take-away.'

'Don't you ever give up?' she said sleepily.

'No. Maybe it's just as well.'

She shuddered. 'Maybe. I'm sorry to be such a nuisance.'

'You're not a nuisance.'

She snuggled closer, her nose pressed against the rough skin of his jaw. She could smell smoke and soap and the remains of his aftershave. It was comforting and reassuringly familiar, and her eyelids started to droop.

Safe in his arms, she let herself slide into oblivion.

CHAPTER SIX

'WELL, I suppose looking on the bright side, it's saved me having to turn out the cupboards, but I didn't realise Joe would go to such lengths to avoid tidying his room!'

Matt looked at the tight smile on Georgia's stricken face and ached for her. She was being so brave about it, but she was hanging by a thread, and he could see why. The bedrooms were seriously damaged. Only a detailed inspection once it was clear would decide how much damage there had been.

'It could have been much worse,' he reminded her. 'You're all OK, that's what matters.'

'I know.'

She cast another despairing look around Joe's bedroom, at the charred remains of his furniture and the gaping hole in the ceiling where the rafters had caught, and went out, picking her way carefully across the landing to the stairs.

He followed her down, avoiding the soot-streaked banisters with their blistered paint, breathing in the bitter smell of wet ash. It was like tramping through an old bonfire, he thought.

The sitting room was ruined by the fallen ceiling, soggy sheets of plasterboard sagging down across the furniture over the firemen's plastic sheeting. Ornaments were smashed, little treasures that she picked up and shed silent, controlled tears over.

It wasn't like her to be so controlled, so passionless. Matt wanted to take her away, to shield her from it, but he knew he couldn't. She went out of the sitting room and into the kitchen, streaked with soot and stinking of wet smoke, like the rest.

'This should clean up,' he told her, but she didn't seem to be comforted. She moved on, through the sodden hall squelching with the filthy water on the floor, through to the studio in her converted double garage.

It was hardly touched, except for the smuts and soot lying over everything, and he watched as she went through, picking up ruined pieces of artwork and putting them down again.

'Thank God I got the *Red Book* and the project out,' she murmured. 'I think the smoke did more damage than the fire.'

'It usually does.'

'I know. Really there's very little in here that's lost— the paperwork in the filing cabinets is all safe, at least. That means I've got the insurance policy.'

She shuddered, rubbing her hands over her arms in a way that was becoming familiar to him. She did it when she felt stressed or insecure, and right now, he imagined, she must be feeling both.

'We'll have to find somewhere to live—I was hoping it would be a case of cleaning up and moving back in, but it's not, is it?' she said, turning to him with eyes wide with realisation. She swallowed. 'It's going to have to be stripped out and rewired and redecorated, and the roof done—good grief, it almost needs to be rebuilt. It could take months!'

'You can stay with me,' he said, without thinking, without hesitation. There was nothing to think about. They were more than welcome.

'I can't,' she protested. 'You've got a life to lead— and anyway, I need to find somewhere where I can set up the business until the house is sorted out. We can't work here, not until the builders have finished. There won't be any electricity or water.'

She drifted back to the sitting room, eyes scanning the damage in disbelief. She reminded him of television pictures of refugees, people dispossessed by war and famine and natural disasters, picking over the pieces of their lives in despair.

'I've got a cottage—it's a converted coach house, just near the top of the drive, and I lived there while the house was being repaired. It's small, but it's totally self contained and at the moment it's empty. You're welcome to it for as long as you need.'

She swivelled slowly, taking in his words one by one. 'Empty?'

'Yes. You can move in as soon as you like—today, if you want.'

'What about rent? I think the policy pays out for accommodation.'

He shrugged. 'Whatever. I don't want any rent for it, so if you can get it back, you might as well pocket the profit.'

She fingered the smoke-blackened remains of her three piece suite. 'Is it furnished?' she asked quietly.

'Yes—it's all ready to move into.'

'There's still the problem of the studio,' she said. 'I should find somewhere where we can work and live, otherwise I have to take the children with me or get babysitters.'

'The barn where we keep the microlight is in two halves—the other half is weather-tight and done out as a games room. We could move the snooker table to one end and you could have that. It's got power and water—it's not attached to the coach house, but it's not far—

just across the yard. Would that do, just in the short term?'

'I'd have to rent it—I can't just take your charity.'

She was going to be stubborn, he thought. How typical of her. 'It's not charity, it's self-interest,' he said firmly. 'If I've got you on the spot, I can pester you about the garden. Anyway, it's not doing anything, you might as well have it.'

She bit her lip, gnawing at it so hard he thought it must hurt.

'I don't know—'

'Just say yes,' he said gently, giving in to his urge and taking her into his arms. 'You've had enough to cope with. Just let me do this for you, get you over this crisis.'

She leant back, staring up at him with puzzled eyes. 'Why should you want to?' she asked.

He looked at her, so sad, so tired, so devastated by the loss of her home, and wondered how she thought he could do anything else. 'I just do,' he told her, kissing her lightly on her poor, bruised lips. 'Now, find that insurance policy, and we'll ring the company and get everything under way.'

It took two days, but finally she and the children were installed in the coach house, and Terry and Mick and Sal had helped her relocate the studio, with the aid of Matt's Discovery and the big box trailer he used to transport the microlight.

Her possessions were in two places. Some had gone to be professionally cleaned, to get the dreadful smell of smoke out of them, and the rest were packed up and stored in one of the many rooms in the house that Matt didn't need.

He'd worked tirelessly alongside them, she thought, and without his kindness and powers of organisation it would have been much harder.

Now she sat back in a comfortable chair in the little sitting room of the coach house, soft music playing on the stereo system in the corner, a nicely chilled glass of wine in her hand, and regarded him thoughtfully over the top of the glass.

'Why have you done all this for me?' she asked, still puzzled by his kindness.

He gave a short laugh. 'Is it so impossible to believe that I wanted to do it for you? That I would have done it for anyone in your position?'

She looked down. 'I'm sorry. I just don't know anyone else who would bother.'

'I'm not Brian.'

She looked up again, startled. 'What?'

'I said, I'm not Brian. Stop comparing me to him.'

Her glass was suddenly fascinating. She swirled the wine, wondering how he managed to read her mind every time, sometimes even before she did. 'I'm sorry. I didn't realise that I was, but you're probably right. He never did anything for anyone without some sort of return on his investment.'

'I'm sure, and it's made you suspicious. All the time, you're waiting for the payback. You're waiting for me to say, "I've given you this, now you give me that." Aren't you?'

'But you have,' she said, remembering the business of the rent. 'You wouldn't let me pay for this place— you said pocket the money and you could pester me about the garden.'

'I was joking. I don't intend to pester you,' he assured her. 'I just didn't want you to worry about money.

Invoice me for the work, if you'd rather, and I can knock the rent off the bill, but it will muddy the waters with my accountant and get me in trouble.'

Did she believe him? He was an investment analyst. Did they even *have* accountants? Maybe if Brian had had one, he wouldn't have got into the mess he had—

'Tell me about your marriage,' he said softly, changing the subject.

She met his eyes, not sure she could bare her soul to him, and found nothing there but kindness and understanding.

'I was far too young,' she began. 'He was twenty-four, I was nineteen. I married him and finished my college course, and then he told me he wanted me to stay at home and run the flat. It didn't need running—it was tiny, there were only two of us—so I did a little work on the side, garden designs for show houses, that sort of thing. He never knew about it. Then, suddenly, there were three of us, and he began to change.'

'Was Joe planned?'

She shook her head. 'No. I had no intention of having a baby when I was that young. I was only just twenty two when he was born, hardly more than a baby myself, but of course I felt very grown up. I joined an organisation for young mothers, and it was fun meeting all the other mums and comparing notes.'

She fell silent, remembering Brian's anger when he'd found out.

'What happened?'

'He came home one day when the group was meeting at our flat. He went wild, threw them all out, almost literally. He told me there was no way his flat was going to be used as some kind of crèche. I never saw any of them again.'

His mouth tightened, and he turned his wine glass thoughtfully in his fingers. 'So what happened then?'

'I was very lonely,' she told him, remembering the long days in the flat with only Joe for company. 'Isolated. Joe was lovely, but I was desperate for another adult to talk to.

'I went out to a toddler group once a week, and we walked in the park and fed the ducks and all those sorts of things. Then I became pregnant again, and I felt too ill to do anything. I still had to entertain, though—as you know. It was better by the time you came for drinks. At least I'd stopped feeling so sick.'

'Did he hit you because the tonic water wasn't cold enough?'

His mouth was tight, his eyes hard with anger at the man who had made her cry. She looked away, reluctant to remember, unable to forget.

'Yes,' she told him quietly. 'Yes, he hit me. Only that once. I told him if he ever did it again we were leaving, and he wouldn't ever see his son again. That frightened him. He couldn't cope without me, he said, and he begged me not to leave. Like a fool I stayed.'

'And was it better?'

'In a way. After that he just resorted to verbal abuse. He was good at it, and he got lots of practice, but I learned to ignore him. I started work again, from home, putting the drawing board away before he came in each night, so he never knew, and gradually I built up a name for myself.'

'And he never found out?'

'Oh, he did in the end. I won an award, and the story broke. I thought he'd kill me, at first.' She laughed bitterly. 'Then, of course, he thought it was wonderful because I was in one of the big Sunday papers. His wife, the successful garden designer. You'd think he'd won the award himself.' She stood up, unfolding her legs and wincing. 'More wine?' she suggested.

'Thanks.' He handed her his glass, his eyes watchful, and she took the glasses out to the kitchen and filled them up. She didn't normally drink very much, but tonight she thought she might make an exception. It had been a hell of a few days, and just this once she needed to let go.

'Here.' She put the glass back into his hand and curled into her chair again. 'Where was I?'

'In the Sunday papers.'

'Oh, yes.' She thought of that time, of the next two years with Brian getting more and more abusive, more and more extravagant and yet somehow meaner, as if he only spent money if it would show. She'd had to use her own money for the housekeeping, but he wouldn't talk about it.

'I think money ruined him. He was all right at first, but over the years it corrupted him and changed him. Actually I think it frightened him. He couldn't cope with it. By the end he'd do anything for kicks—anything for an adrenaline rush. He took bigger and bigger risks on the futures market, bigger risks everywhere.

'That was why he died—parascending in the Mediterranean, crashing into rocks because they'd all been drinking since breakfast. And then, of course, I found out what a hollow sham it all was, and how broke we really were.'

His brow creased. 'Broke?'

She laughed. 'Oh, yes. We had nothing. It was terrifying how everything suddenly collapsed around us. The flat was rented, the furniture was on contract hire, the Mercedes was on HP and the payments were overdue—

the only thing he'd done was take out a small life insurance policy, and I used it to buy the house—'

She ground to a halt, remembering the ashes of her investment, and shook her head despairingly. 'I thought we were sorted out now. I'd found my feet, my work was coming together, I was getting real recognition— and now this, everything reduced to ashes.'

He stood up, coming over and crouching in front of her, taking her hands in his. 'Not everything. You're all right, and the children are all right, and although you've lost some things they're only material possessions. You've still got your memories, and you've got the photos of the children. At least you had insurance, you can start again.'

He was right. She smiled, grateful to him for reminding her of how lucky they'd been. 'I know. Thanks. I tend to forget the insurance. I keep panicking.'

'Silly girl.' He bent closer and dropped a kiss on her forehead. 'I'm going—unless I'm about to get an offer I can't refuse?'

She laughed softly and shook her head. 'No—sorry. You wouldn't want me. I'm hot and sweaty and I stink of smoke. I need a hot bath, an early night and a late start in the morning. Then I might be civilised.'

He chuckled and stood up. 'Right. I'm off. Sleep well.'

She followed him to the door, meaning everything she'd just said and yet unwilling to let him go. 'Matt?'

He looked down at her, his eyes gentle. 'Yes?'

'Thanks for everything. You've been wonderful.'

He said nothing, just leant down and pressed a quick, hard kiss to her lips, then turning on his heel he strode off across the yard and round the side of the barn, whistling for Murphy as he went. The dog bounded up beside him, a grey wraith in the fading light, and she watched them out of sight before closing the door, a faint smile on her lips.

He was a good man, she thought. If only she could work out his motives...

It was amazing how quickly they settled into the new living and working environment. The barn was wonderful, much bigger than the converted double garage they'd been struggling with, and they enjoyed working in the countryside with the doors and windows open and the outside coming in. It was strange, but they all seemed more creative, more productive as a result.

The children were at school, of course, and seemed to have got over the fire without any problems. Joe was the more troubled of the two, but she thought guilt probably played a large part in that, and she made sure he knew she didn't blame him, and gradually he seemed to relax again.

The London client was finally happy with the design, and so the builders were commissioned to do the hard landscaping. So much for that.

Now, Chelsea. The show was on the following week, and she needed to buy a ticket. There was an interesting programme on the television on Friday evening, showing the run-down to the opening, the hard work and preparation, the nail-biting worries over whether the plants would all peak at the right time.

She watched it avidly, feeling the little surge of adrenaline on their behalf, and on her own behalf for the following year. Britain's most prestigious flower show, and she was going to be exhibiting.

Oh, Lord!

Her phone rang, just at the end of the programme, and she picked it up. It was Matt.

'How do you fancy going to Chelsea?' he said, echoing her thoughts. He must have been watching it, too.

'I'm going,' she told him.

'On Monday night?'

'Gala night?' she said with a laugh. 'It costs a fortune, and you have to book tickets in September. They sell out in forty-eight hours—'

'I've got two tickets.'

Her jaw dropped, and she plopped onto the arm of the chair and stared at the receiver. 'What?' she said, her voice a squeak.

'I said, I've got two tickets—'

'I heard that. I mean—how?'

'I'm a man of power and influence,' he said, a thread of laughter in his voice. 'Actually, it's a hospitality do— a client I've advised. Let's just say he owed me. I thought you might like to go. We could stay overnight and go to Members' Day the next day—see who the medal winners are.'

She thought of the fun of the evening party, with all the Royals in attendance, the champagne and the glitter, and then the opportunity to see the gardens without the awful crush of the crowds on the public days, to talk to the designers and the medal winners. She knew several of the people doing gardens this year. It would be helpful to get a little inside information.

And then she thought of the cost—the dress and jacket or whatever, suitable for mingling with the rich and famous—you couldn't just turn up in the jeans you were wearing when your house burned down!

And then the hotel bill—and he hadn't said much about that, but she had a sneaking feeling it would be one room—the payback, if you like, for the tickets—and the worst thing was, she felt tempted.

'Georgia? You still there?'

'I'm not sure,' she said slowly. 'Why do you want to go?'

'Because I love gardens? Because I know you're interested and it's always more fun going with someone who knows what they're talking about?'

'It just costs so much—I can't afford the clothes, for a start, and then there's the hotel bill, and—'

'Can I come round?'

'Um—yes, of course.'

The children were in bed, they could talk about it—maybe if she could see his eyes she'd be able to judge better exactly what he was up to.

He was there in moments, a bottle of wine in one hand, a box of dark chocolate truffles in the other.

'Here—a snack while we chat.' He grinned disarmingly, and she felt a flutter of—what? Panic? Excitement? Something, anyway, that made her heart beat strangely and her legs go weak.

She took the chocolates and put them on the table, then handed him two glasses and a corkscrew. 'Here—you can be all hunky with the wine while I open the chocolates,' she said with a smile, and sat down quickly before her legs gave way.

What was it about him that did that to her?

He passed her a glass of wine, took a chocolate and settled himself down in the chair opposite her, then started ticking things off on his fingers.

'Right, let's start at the top. You need a dress or a suit or something—nothing flashy, just the sort of thing you probably need in your wardrobe anyway, and probably had—so claim it on your insurance. Sensible shoes so you can walk round and enjoy it—I'm sure you've got those, or need them.'

'What about the hotel? I can't let you pay for that—'

'No hotel bill. We'll stay with my parents—they live in Richmond. They'll be delighted to have us.'

His parents? Good grief. That should be safe, anyway.

'Well?' he prompted.

'The children,' she said, belatedly coming to her senses. 'I'd need to find someone to look after them. Jenny, perhaps—'

'They could stay with Mr and Mrs Hodges in their cottage. They seem to spend a lot of time in there with them anyway, I'm sure they'd feel at home.'

'Oh, but I couldn't ask them—'

'I already have, and they said yes.' He took another sip of wine and regarded her steadily over the rim. 'Well?' he repeated.

'Lovely,' she said weakly. He'd scotched all her arguments at a stroke, and anyway, she didn't want to talk herself out of it! She was dying to go, and a little fizzle of excitement was starting in the bottom of her stomach.

'So you will come?'

She nodded. 'Please. It sounds wonderful.'

He gave a self-satisfied smile, clearly pleased with himself. 'Excellent. Right, you'd better go shopping tomorrow and sort your dress out. Do you need any money? I can lend you some if you're short until the insurance is sorted out.'

She shook her head. 'No—don't worry. I'm fine. They gave me a cheque to take care of immediate expenditure—that can be part of it!' She smiled, and helped herself to another truffle. Now that was out of the way, she could settle down to the serious business of eating the chocolates!

*   *   *

Gala night was glorious, a fabulous evening, warm and sunny, fading into a beautiful clear, starlit night.

They arrived at seven, Matt in a dark suit and startlingly white shirt, Georgia in a new dress, soft and flowing, a silk mixture with enough of something else in it to give it body and enough silk to make it flow like water.

It was patterned, unusually for her, a smother of flowers in muted pastels in a watercolour print that looked as if it had been painted while the cloth was wet.

The colours were perfect for her, balancing her red hair, bringing out the clear tones of her skin, and she was thrilled to bits with it. It swirled round her legs as she moved, and she felt sensuous and elegant and beautiful.

The only fly in the ointment was Matt, and he was being fairly non-committal about it. He had looked her up and down, said, when she'd asked if it was all right, that it was absolutely fine, and that was it.

She was disappointed, but what had she expected? A declaration of love? It was only a dress, after all, and maybe it was because they'd been in a hurry. They had arrived at his parents' house with just enough time to say hello, change and rush out, so perhaps she was expecting too much.

She had hoped for a more dynamic response, though, and all her old insecurities came back as they walked down to the hospitality chalet that was hosting their evening.

'Are you sure my dress is all right?' she asked again, checking the other guests anxiously.

He stopped in his tracks, turned to her and gave a grim smile. 'You look beautiful, Georgia. I'm having trouble keeping my hands off you. All I want to do is drag you off behind the nearest tent and ravish you. Is that better?'

She laughed softly. 'Much. Thank you.'

He chuckled, and hugged her against his side. 'You do look beautiful. I adore the dress, but I wish it didn't have buttons all the way down the front. I'm fighting the urge to unbutton it.'

She felt colour flood her cheeks, and moved away from him. 'Down, boy,' she said softly, and thought it was probably both a shame and a pity that they were staying with his parents—in quite definitely separate rooms!

They sipped champagne, looked through their 'goody bags' of programme and map and little samples of this and that, and then after the Royal party left the grounds at seven-thirty, they were able to look round.

'We've only got an hour—what do you want to see first?' he asked her.

'The show gardens,' she said promptly, and they made their way first to the rock garden bank, where the sloping gardens were situated. Georgia was fascinated. She wanted to examine each garden, to climb over the fence and walk round, touching, smelling, revelling in the stunning attention to detail that was the hallmark of every garden.

Matt kept moving her on, knowing she wanted to see them all, chivvying her so she didn't run out of time before they had to go back to the tent for dinner.

'I don't want to eat, I just want to look,' she wailed at eight-thirty, when he suggested they should go back. So they strolled slowly, enjoying the fact that there were no crowds and that they could see the gardens, and then they were back in the tent, tucking into the buffet, because despite what she'd said, she was actually starving!

They left at ten, went back to his parents' and chatted in the kitchen until midnight, then he took her upstairs, kissed her goodnight and left her at her bedroom door.

She rather wished he hadn't, but she slept like a log, probably because of the liberal champagne, and had to be dragged out of bed at six thirty so they could be back there before eight.

The medal winners were looking delighted, still in the first flush of excitement having been allowed in at seven to see the result of the judging and hopefully, if they'd been lucky, find a card with the embossed medal pinned on their garden or exhibit.

There were surprises, and she and Matt were both proved wrong on what they'd felt were dead certs. The overall winner, though, was only slightly more deserving than some of the others, and they disagreed both with each other and the judges on which was the best, laughingly wrangling over the result.

She had a wonderful day, and to his eternal credit Matt trailed along behind her, feeding her at intervals and carrying bags of garden brochures, free samples, packets of seed and other little things she'd had to buy.

'You must be bored to death,' she said at last, turning to look at him as they left yet another stand that she'd found riveting.

He smiled wryly. 'Not bored, exactly. Just stunned that you know so much about it all. I thought I knew a bit about gardens, but I now realise I know nothing. I feel very humble.'

'I'm sorry,' she said, instantly contrite, but he smiled and hugged her.

'Don't be sorry. I'm learning all the time. Maybe some of it will sink in.'

'Tell me when you want to go,' she said firmly, awash with guilt. 'I'm just being self-indulgent now.'

'I'm fine. You carry on. We're here for you—we'll go when you're ready.'

They went, in the end, because her feet gave out, and arrived back at Heveling at midnight. The children were spending another night at the Hodges', and he took her home, turned her into his arms in the hall and kissed her till her blood sang in her veins.

'Thank you so much,' she said a little breathlessly when he finally let her go. 'It's been the most wonderful two days. I don't know how to repay you.'

'Who said anything about being repaid, and what for? The pleasure of your company? Don't be silly.'

He kissed her again, then eased away. 'I'm going now. Lock the door. I'll see you tomorrow.'

She watched him go, then locked up, slid into bed and curled herself round her pillow with a contented sigh. Her feet ached, her legs felt heavy, her mind was whirling—and Matt was the most wonderful man in the world.

Whatever did he see in her?

CHAPTER SEVEN

THE trouble with going to Chelsea, Georgia mused, was that it gave you so many new ideas, sparked so many new avenues of thought. In the week following the show she flicked through her sketches and designs for her own submission—the outline sketch submitted to the Royal Horticultural Society for approval, the draft planting plan, the hard landscaping ideas she'd had.

She didn't like it. It seemed too stilted, somehow—too perfect. It was a very clean design, and she liked chaos. Still, it was the sponsor's design brief, and his money.

She made a few changes, dreamed up some costings, rang her sponsor and discussed the level of funding, and got tentative approval. Wonderful. Now all she had to do was make sure everything was sorted out in time to submit the final plan to the RHS in the autumn, once she knew which plot she'd been allocated.

Which left Matt's garden.

She wandered out of the barn and over to the walled garden, letting herself in and strolling quietly round the edge, getting the feel. It was lovely. The roses were starting to come out, and one by one she was identifying them and noting them down on her plan.

They had such evocative names—*Rosa gallica officinalis*, the Apothecary's rose, used for hundreds of years in herbal medicines, the huge crimson flowers beautifully scented; *Rosa Mundi*, boldly striped crimson and white, another ancient rose; Quatre Saisons, clear

pink, wonderfully scented, repeat flowering; York and
Lancaster, with pink and white blooms on the same
bush; Celestial and Maiden's Blush, both over four hundred years old—they were wonderful, tough, disease-
free bushes, with none of the tendency of modern roses
to succumb to rust or mildew.

She wondered how old the bushes were, and thought
it quite probable, looking at the thick stems and unruly
habit, that they were original, planted by men employed
to carry out the wishes of Humphrey Repton. It made
her hair stand on end just to think about it.

Some, of course, were just a mass of suckers coming
up from the rootstock and had reverted to briars. They,
sadly, would have to come out, but the ones that had
survived were a real treasure-trove, and she took cuttings
and potted them up in the tumble-down greenhouse
she'd found in the old walled kitchen garden beyond the
rose garden.

Matt found her there, dabbling in compost and humming happily, and handed her a glass of iced tea beaded
with moisture on the outside.

She smiled and took it, draining it instantly. It was
hot work in the greenhouse. She gave him another smile
as she set the glass down. 'Thanks. I was coming in for
a drink in a moment, but I got sidetracked.'

'You love it, don't you?' He propped himself up
against the old wooden staging and studied her with a
quizzical smile. 'Pottering about amongst your plants.
That's what you're happiest doing.'

She laughed and patted the compost down around her
cuttings, then watered them in. 'My secrets are found
out,' she agreed. 'Plants are so tough, so willing to survive. So long as we give them the basic essentials, they
seem to live almost to spite us. Do you know some of

your rose bushes are probably nearly two hundred years old?'

He nodded. 'I'm not surprised. Are those cuttings of them?'

'Hopefully. It isn't always easy with roses, but it's often better to clone than to graft. You get a truer result, and of course that way we'd get the same tough genes that have kept these roses alive for such a long time. You should really do it in November, but these might take.'

'And the parterre? How are the plans coming on?'

She shrugged away from the staging and headed for the door. 'Come and see. We've marked out the corners of the square with white posts, but we could do with an aerial view to make sure they're in the right place before we go any further—if you're that fussy.'

He nodded. 'Sure. It would be nice to get it right. So, when are we going up?'

She laughed. '*We* aren't,' she told him firmly. 'You can go whenever you like—take Terry, my designer. He'd love it, he's an idiot and he'd probably like a break from the drawing board. Do you have a radio that would work?'

'No—it's too loud to communicate clearly. We can design some signals, though. You could stand on the ground and we could fly in the direction you need to move. We should only have to do it a couple of times, and the rest would follow, if you and Humphrey Repton had the same tape measure.'

'If,' she said with a chuckle. 'OK. Let's try it.'

Amazingly, it worked. They were pretty accurate, it turned out, but just a foot or so too far from the house, and a little longer than the original. She marked the centre, as well, and then they disappeared over the horizon with a waggle of wings.

So Terry, obviously, didn't suffer from motion sickness the way she did. Either that or he wasn't going to be fit for work for days!

She banged in the markers, checked the measurements and found they were true. So far so good. Now, all they needed was to plot out the lines of the little hedges, and they could begin the planting.

She fetched string, and sand to mark the lines, and took Sal away from her visuals to help her, and between them they had most of the first segment marked out by the time Matt and Terry came back. They came through the gateway laughing and waving their arms, and clearly had had a great time.

Georgia shook her head. 'Mad, both of you,' she said with a smile. 'Have fun?'

'Excellent,' Terry agreed, eyes glowing. 'It's really easy to fly—I had the controls for a while. Wicked.'

'You must be nuts.'

'No, it's great. We've been to Felixstowe and Harwich and all along the coast,' Terry told her, still bubbling.

'On my time,' she said repressively, but he just grinned.

'Make up for all the overtime I put in out of love, won't it?'

She had to squash the smile. 'Hmm. Well, anyway, how does this look? Sal and I have been hard at work while you two have been gallivanting around the place!'

Matt nodded. 'Looks good. Perhaps you need to look from the old drawing room—the view's better from the roof, but I don't suppose I can talk you out onto that either, can I?'

'Not in this lifetime,' she agreed. 'However, I can

cope with the drawing room. Terry, could you and Sal
go and finish off the visuals for Mrs Baker? And then
she's out of the way and we can concentrate on Chelsea
for a while. If this looks right we can carry on with it
later.'

They went up to the old drawing room, standing at
the window and looking down at what had once been a
formal and elegant complement to the room. Now, it was
a weedy, lumpy mess with lines on it, but the lines
seemed to be in the right place.

'You can see the grass is just a little darker on the
hedge lines,' she said, squinting to cut out most of the
light so the contrast was easier to see. 'I don't think we'll
get it any better than that.'

'You could always check it yourself,' he teased.

She laughed. 'You know quite well I'll go up in that
ghastly instrument for neither love nor money, so you
might as well save your breath,' she told him. 'Anyway,
you said it was all right.'

'It was.' He turned his back to the window, leaning
on the glass and folding his arms. 'So. What are you
doing tonight?'

'Marking out the parterre? Drawing up the next draft
for Chelsea? Washing clothes?'

'Letting me cook you dinner?'

'I have the children.'

'Mrs Hodges will babysit.'

'She might not be able to.'

'She can. I asked.'

'Before you asked me?' She tried to sound cross.
'Taking it for granted, aren't you?'

He gave her that lovely cock-eyed smile. 'Not at all.
Just making sure of my options.'

She weakened. She hadn't spent any real time with him since Chelsea, and she missed him.

'What are you cooking?' she asked, as if it mattered.

'Lobster. I happen to have been given one earlier today.'

'Is it still alive?' she asked, a touch squeamish. She didn't like her food on the hoof, so to speak. It made her feel guilty, but she adored lobster.

'No, it's cooked. I was going to do it with a mustard mayonnaise, and salad. And there might be Mrs Hodges' chocolate pavlova for supper,' he added craftily, knowing chocolate was her weakness.

'I'm convinced,' she said with a smile, 'but only if you let me pay Mrs Hodges for her time.'

'Done,' he said, too quickly for her to trust him. He'd probably already paid her, the sneaky rat.

'What time?'

'Eight? That gives you plenty of time to put the children to bed and read to them and so forth.'

She nodded. 'Good. Thanks. I ought to go and sort the others out now. I'll see you at eight.'

They wandered downstairs and parted at the kitchen door. She turned back and said, as an afterthought, 'Are we dressing?'

He laughed, a soft, wicked chuckle that teased his eyes. 'Now, there's a lovely idea. What if I say no?'

'You know what I mean,' she said, pretending to be stern. 'Am I dressing up?'

'Do you want to?' he asked, reminding her abruptly of the sparsity of her wardrobe since the fire.

'It's a bit tricky,' she admitted. 'Clean jeans and a jumper is about the limit—unless I wear the Chelsea dress.'

His eyes darkened. 'That will be just perfect—unless you want to plump for the other option of not dressing?'

'I think not,' she said with a dry chuckle, and left him, propped against the door frame, that wicked smile playing on his lips.

The food was wonderful. He'd prepared the lobster to perfection, and managed to talk Mrs Hodges into making her chocolate pavlova with strawberries and cream, and yet they ate in the kitchen, with Murphy asleep in the corner and Scally purring on top of the fridge.

Georgia ate without thought for her figure, starving hungry after a busy day outside, and then as she finished she sat back and smiled.

'Wow. That was wonderful. Thank you.'

He smiled. 'Thank *you*. It's good to see a woman eat properly and not just pick at her food. I can't stand that.'

'Nor me. I can always go on a diet tomorrow.'

'Now, why would you want to do that? You've got a lovely figure.'

She felt colour brush her cheeks. 'Don't be silly,' she murmured.

'I'm not. I mean it. You're beautiful, Georgia—warm and funny and colourful and a real delight.'

The colour heightened. 'You're going too far now,' she said softly. 'I might be funny, but the others—'

'And argumentative. Why do you always have to have the last word?'

He stood up and drew her to her feet. 'Come up to the drawing room. I'll put the coffee on, and while we wait we can dance.'

'Dance?' she said, trailing after him with her heart pounding against her ribs.

'Yes, dance. That dress is too beautiful to waste.'

He meant it. She couldn't dance with him—not to-night, when he was being so funny and relaxed. It was too dangerous, too easy to fall under his spell—

He put on the lights, just the soft glow of the table lamps, and with a touch to the remote control the room was flooded with music.

Romantic, seductive music—music for lovers.

And Georgia knew she was in deep, deep trouble—

'Come here,' he murmured, and she went into his arms without a word of protest.

It seemed a waste of time to argue, because he'd win anyway. She wanted him to, apart from anything else, and besides, it was only a dance.

Then she stopped analysing it in her head and concentrated on enjoying it, enjoying him—the way he could tuck her head under his chin, so that her ear lay against the steady beat of his heart; the way his arms felt so strong, so sure around her, and yet she knew if she moved away, he'd let her go.

Her body seemed so in tune with him that she anticipated every move. They seemed to flow together, so that she lost track of where she ended and he began. They were like one, swaying together to the sultry music, separated only by a thin layer of clothes and her rapidly dwindling reluctance.

She felt his lips brush her forehead, the soft scrape of his beard against her skin tantalising her. She lifted her head, tipping it back to give him access as his lips skimmed over her jaw and settled on the tender skin of her throat, and a low grunt of satisfaction rumbled from his chest.

'So beautiful,' he whispered against her throat. He pushed aside the neck of her dress, slipping open the first button, and laid hot, open-mouthed kisses down over the creamy slope of her breast.

She whimpered, and he lifted his head and cradled her against his chest again. His lips pressed against her hair, and his hands locked behind her back and held her lightly against him. They weren't moving now, just standing together, listening to the sensual songs and letting the flames between them die down a little.

Eventually he lifted his head, and she realised that the music had stopped, and the only thing she could hear was the steady, rhythmic beat of his heart.

'Coffee?' he murmured, and she nodded, unwilling to release him even for that long.

She went with him to the kitchen to retrieve the tray, and then they went back up to the drawing room and sat on one of the huge, comfy old sofas that bracketed the fireplace. 'Black or white?' he asked.

'White—thanks.' She took the cup, a delicate bone-china beaker with roses scrambling all over it, and sipped appreciatively. It was lovely, the cream cool on the surface, and the coffee had a kick that spread heat through her and left a mellow tide in its wake.

'You've spiked it,' she accused him mildly, and he smiled.

'Me? Surely not.' He lounged back into the corner, looking sexy and dangerous and boy-next-door all at once, and she had an overwhelming urge to throw away her inhibitions and allow things to take their course. He'd made it quite obvious he'd welcome an affair, and at the moment, it seemed that everyone was losing. If she gave in, changed her mind, then what harm would it do?

She was the only one who'd be hurt by it. He'd already made it clear he wasn't in it for the long haul, on

their picnic a few weeks ago, so it was hardly going to
break his heart when he decided to move on.

The children could be kept out of his way to save
them growing more fond of him, and that left her.

And what, exactly, was she gaining from her sacrifice?

Nothing. She was lonely, life was a trial at the moment, and she knew that making love with Matt would
be wonderful. So what was stopping her? What exactly
was she saving herself for?

'Penny for them.'

She laughed a little wildly. 'Not on your life,' she
said, and took a gulp of her coffee. The Irish whiskey
in it burned its way down her throat, and she blinked
and swallowed.

'That must have been some thought,' he said with a
chuckle, and she felt colour scorch her cheeks.

'Wouldn't you like to know?'

'Absolutely. Come here, you're too far away.'

She put her cup down and moved closer, and he
wrapped his arm round her shoulders and eased her
down against his side. His head lolled against the back
of the sofa, and he propped his feet on the coffee table
and sighed gently. 'This is nice,' he said lazily. 'I feel
like Scally—well fed, pampered and utterly content.'

'Let's just hope the dog doesn't chase you up the barn,
then,' Georgia said with a chuckle.

His chest shook under her ear, and his arm tightened
momentarily. 'You are lovely,' he said quietly, and then
he shifted so that her shoulders were against the back of
the sofa and his head was above her, looking down with
a strange expression on his face.

Thoughtful and pensive and—yes, longing.

She reached up a hand and touched him, cupping his

cheek and drawing his face down to hers. Surrender
ing...

She looked beautiful lying there in his bed, he thought.
Even more beautiful than he'd imagined her.

Typically Georgia, she hadn't been sweetly respon-
sive, but wild and generous and honest. His body tightened at the thought, and he turned from the window to
look at her again.

It seemed a shame to wake her, but Mrs Hodges
would be wanting to go home and it was nearly midnight. He had taken the precaution of pulling on his
clothes, because he knew one touch of her lips and he
would be in the bed beside her again, powerless to resist.

He sat beside her, and she stirred as the mattress
dipped. 'Georgia—wake up, sweetheart. Time to go
home.'

Her eyes fluttered lazily open and she stared at him
for a long moment, then smiled, her eyes soft with memories. 'I thought it was a dream,' she confessed.

He laughed softly. 'Some dream.'

'They have been,' she confessed, 'but not that good.
Reality was better.'

'I know the feeling.' He pulled down the sheets and
studied her, the soft, creamy swell of her breasts, the
dusky pink nipples, the dip of her navel. 'Gorgeous,' he
murmured. 'Exquisite. Damn, I don't want you to go.'

She reached up her hand and touched his lips, tracing
the outline with one of her slender, work-roughened little
fingers. 'Kiss me one more time,' she murmured.

It was well after midnight by the time he walked her
home.

Georgia kissed him goodbye on the cheek, because Mrs
Hodges was hovering with a rapt look on her face, ob-

viously aching for romance.

Georgia asked about the children, paid her and then closed the door, leaning against it and hugging her arms around her waist.

She'd had no idea it could be like that—wild, passionate, tender, earthily physical and yet somehow almost touched by angels—

Oh, she was going mad, getting into the realms of dreadful poetry!

I love him, she thought with shock, and chewed her lip. Fool. Still, she realised now she'd loved him before, so it was no big deal. She just loved him more now—knew better who it was she was loving.

She went to bed, but not until she'd visited the bathroom and caught sight of herself in the mirror. Who did she think she was fooling, kissing him on the cheek? she thought hysterically, and crushed the bubble of laughter that rose in her throat.

She looked well and truly loved. Her lips were swollen from his kisses, her hair was tousled and her eyes—Lord alone knows what's happened to my eyes, she thought. They were glazed, with that sleepy, contented look that came from absolute bliss.

She touched her lips, still feeling the lingering warmth of his mouth, the hunger of his kisses. Oh, Matt, she thought tenderly. She slipped into bed, curled on her side and ached to hold him. Was he feeling the same, his arms empty, his heart full?

She'd see him tomorrow—just eight hours or so.

Suddenly it seemed like for ever.

The next few days were ecstasy. By day she worked on her designs or his garden, and every day he found an

excuse to spend an hour or two alone with her.
Sometimes they just had lunch in the garden. At other
times, when they could steal longer, they went upstairs
and closed the door of his bedroom and revelled in their
new-found intimacy.

And by night, when the children were in bed asleep,
he would come round and bring a bottle of wine, and
they'd share it in front of the television or listening to
music, or just talking, curled up on the chairs in the little
sitting room, with Murphy lying at his feet.

And then one day her bliss was shattered, because she
had a phone call from her Chelsea sponsor to say he was
pulling out.

'Our profits are down, Georgia, and we can't justify
it,' he told her. 'I'm sorry. You'll have to find another
sponsor, if you can. The RHS might be able to help.'

And that was that. No sponsor, no Chelsea.

She thought of all the work that had gone into it, all
the planning and worrying and lack of sleep, and she
thought she was going to explode.

With a muttered excuse to the others, she went out,
crossed the yard to the gate in the walled garden and
went in, banging the gate behind her. She'd catalogued
the roses, chosen the replacements to put in in the autumn, and now she could start removing those that had
run to suckers or died.

Probably with her bare hands, she was so mad.

Matt found her there some time later, heaving down
on a garden fork that was embedded in two hundred
years' worth of tangled roots, and stood watching her,
hands on hips, a quizzical expression on his face.

'Haven't you got anything to do?' she snapped.

One eyebrow arched eloquently. 'Who bit you?' he
said mildly.

'My sponsor—he's pulled out.' She heaved on the fork again, and with a victorious ping! one of the tines snapped and she sat down on her bottom with a bump.

Matt offered her a hand, but she smacked it aside and scrambled to her feet. 'I can manage,' she growled, attacking the rose again as if she had some personal vendetta against it.

He took the mangled fork from her hands and stuck it in the grass, then took her by the hand and towed her into the kitchen. There he sat her down, poured her a large gin and tonic and turning a chair round, he sat down opposite, his arms folded along the back of the chair, his chin propped on his wrists.

'Tell me all about it,' he said calmly.

'No money,' she said, stabbing her hair viciously with her earth-encrusted fingers. 'He said they've run out of money, and can't afford it. He suggested I contact the RHS!'

'And have you?'

'No, of course not! I have to find my own sponsor. There are dozens of designers looking for sponsorship, not the other way round. Do you have any idea what it costs? Thousands—millions, in some cases! The Fleet Street gardens always run to millions, and so do some of the others. I had a six-figure budget from my defaulting sponsor. Where the hell am I going to find another sucker like that?'

'Here?' he said quietly.

'Where?' she exploded. 'In sleepy Suffolk? I hardly think so—!'

She stopped in mid-tirade, staring blankly at him. 'You?' she said, stunned.

'Why not? It's good advertising—'

'No,' she said, panic swamping her. She couldn't let

him do it—couldn't be that beholden. 'I can't—thank you, but I can't. What if you get bored with me and change your mind?'

He laughed softly. 'The chances of me getting bored with you are about a million to one—probably less. And anyway, we aren't talking about me, we're talking about the microlight factory. It's brilliant advertising—lots of people who go to Chelsea like toys. I sell toys. Trust me, I'm not a foolish man with my money.'

She snorted. 'Oh, yeah? You're trying to part yourself from a good bit of it without any thought—'

'Not without thought. I've considered it very carefully since we went to Chelsea. It seems quite sensible, really. Show me the designs.'

'You won't like them,' she said, screwing up her nose. 'I don't like them all that much. I'd much rather do something more on the lines of restoration.'

'Can you change the show garden at this stage?' he asked, running his finger through a wet patch on the table and drawing patterns with it.

She'd never even thought of that—she'd been too busy nursing her disappointment. 'I don't know—probably. They'd have to approve it, but—yes, maybe. Why?'

'I thought perhaps you could build in the summer house.'

Her jaw dropped. 'The summer house—what, your summer house? From here? From the garden?'

He nodded. 'Worth a thought, perhaps. It could be taken down brick by brick, rebuilt there and then brought back again. It's falling down anyway—it might be quite fun.'

Her imagination caught fire. 'It could be a restoration project—some of it untouched, perhaps some repaired—

and the garden could be designed to look as if it were undergoing restoration as well—Matt, you're brilliant! I could copy your parterre!'

Then she floundered to a halt. 'Except, of course, that I don't think I can agree.'

'Yes, you can.'

'No, I can't. I need to be independent—'

'Were you independent of your last sponsor?'

'No, of course not,' she agreed, 'but look what happened to him! He ran out of money and had to bottle out. What if that happens to you?'

'I won't run out of money.'

She eyed him steadily, doubt clawing at her. 'Brian used to pretend to have money,' she told him.

'You can talk to my bank manager if you like.'

Hot colour ran up her cheeks. 'Don't be silly.'

'So, if you believe me, why won't you let me sponsor you?'

She chewed her poor lip again—just when she'd thought it was getting better after the fire. 'Do you really think the publicity is worth that much?'

He shrugged. 'Maybe—how much are we talking about?'

To be honest, she wasn't sure how much money they were talking about, but probably the publicity wouldn't hurt—if only the firm could stand the expenditure.

'I don't know. Without a design to work from, I can't work out the costs.'

'Want to work up a few sketches, throw a few ideas around with the rest of the team? Then you could ring the RHS and put the suggestion to them, and we can go from there.'

She hesitated, then sighed. 'Why?' she asked.

'I told you—publicity,' he replied. 'I don't suppose

we'll make money instantly, but it all helps to raise the profile of the firm, and that has spin-offs.'

'But I feel I've forced you into it—'

He laughed softly. 'No, Georgia. Nobody forces me into anything I don't want to do. We're alike in that, at least.'

She weakened, giving him a tiny smile. 'I just feel guilty—'

'Don't. Just say yes.'

'You say that a lot,' she told him.

'You argue a lot.'

She smiled, and gave in.

'Yes,' she said, and wondered if she would regret it.

CHAPTER EIGHT

THE man she spoke to at the Royal Horticultural Society offices the next morning was more than helpful. He sympathised over the loss of her sponsor, and she understood that it was something that happened often.

So at least, then, she wasn't alone.

He told her they also didn't mind, in principle, if as a result of the change of sponsor she had to change her garden design, and so she was able to sit down in the walled garden with a sheaf of paper and sketch the summer house, and the parterre that she'd dreamed up, and the roses—all scaled down, of course, to a Chelsea plot twenty by forty metres!

And there was his little statue, too, which she could build into the design, and a fountain in the centre of the maze, and—the possibilities were limitless and exciting, and her pencil flew over the paper. She drew sheet after sheet of sketches and plans, rough outlines, working guides to help formulate the final design, and then, satisfied she had something to work on, she went back to Terry and dropped them on his drawing board.

'What do you think of these?' she said with a grin, and plopped down beside him on another stool.

He shuffled them, made interested noises that attracted the rest of the team who came and hung over his shoulder, and between them they quickly drew up a slightly less rough plan. Sal put some colour on the sketch of the summer house, scribbled in the lines of the parterre and fountain, put the statue at the end of the brick path, and Georgia scooped up all the bits of paper and went to find Matt.

He wasn't there. 'Try the estate office,' Mrs Hodges said, so she got in her car and drove the long way round, rather than bumping along the bridleways.

He was just leaving, climbing into the Discovery as she turned in, and he got out, slammed the door and strolled over.

'Don't tell me—you've changed your mind,' he said with a wary smile.

She shook her head. 'Nope. I've spoken to the RHS, we can change the design and we've done a few sketches to show you.'

'Great. Let's take them to the pub—it must be lunch-time.'

'Won't Mrs Hodges be expecting you?' she said, concerned.

'No. I get my own lunch. Come on. You can give me a lift, there's no point in taking two cars. Anyway, there's something else I want to ask you about.'

'Sounds ominous,' she said with a laugh, and shifted the drawings off the passenger seat so he could sit down.

'Not ominous. Just a favour. It's slightly connected, I suppose. I've got a microlight promotion weekend coming up next weekend—several people are coming with their other halves, arriving on Saturday morning and leaving on Sunday morning, and during the day they'll be flying and looking round the factory, and in the evening they'll be entertained at the house.'

'And?'

'And I wondered if you'd consider acting as my hostess for the weekend—entertaining the women during the day, and hostessing the evening with me. I'll pay you, of course, and you're allowed to say no.'

'And the children?'

'Mrs Hodges will be busy, of course—what about your friend Jenny? I'd pay her, too, naturally.'

Naturally. I'll pay, therefore it'll happen.

'That was a big sigh,' he said quietly. 'Is that a no?'

'You could have just asked me. I would have done it for nothing, but you have to muddy the waters with money all the time,' she said bluntly.

He blinked in surprise. 'But I wouldn't dream of asking anyone to do it for nothing. It's too much to expect. Why should you do it?'

Because I'm your lover? she wanted to say. Because you love me, and we share things, and it's the sort of things lovers do for each other?

'You've done enough for me,' she said instead. 'I owe you so much—it would be a chance to pay you back.'

'For what?' he said in surprise.

'For the cottage, for the studio, for helping sort out all the stuff after the fire, for taking me to Chelsea and spoiling me to death—all sorts of things, not to mention sponsoring my garden!'

He threw up his hands and laughed. 'OK, fine, do it for nothing if you have to, but will you do it? I'd really appreciate it if you could—and of course it will help to promote your Chelsea sponsor, thus ensuring the security of the funding!'

And so she found herself talked into doing the very thing she'd always vowed she'd never do again.

Damn.

Still, he was sponsoring her, and it might help sales. It was the least she could do.

They arrived at the pub, settled themselves at a table under a tree, and while they waited for their sandwiches to arrive, they sipped alcohol-free lager and looked at the designs.

'I love it,' he said enthusiastically. 'There's a real feeling of tranquillity about it—I can hear the droning of the bees and smell the roses.'

'So you approve?'

'Definitely.'

'What about the cost? Shall I get some quotes from Chelsea landscapers for moving the summer house? They have professional teams who do it all the time—it would be best to use one of them. They know what they have to do.'

'Sure. We'll do it anyway, but you might as well find out so I can shock the accountant into apoplexy—ah, good, our lunch. Eat up. I want to take you back to the house and discuss this weekend, if you've got time.'

'Which weekend is it, actually?' she said, suddenly having a horrible thought. 'Not the one after this?'

'Yes—why, is that a problem?'

She chewed her lip thoughtfully. 'Not if you don't need me on the Friday evening or Sunday afternoon. It's Joe's birthday on Friday, and I ought to do something with him. I thought I might take him out, and then on Sunday he'll want a party—is it all right to do that at the coach house?'

'Of course,' he said instantly. 'Will you have enough room? You could use the barn, if you like. I'll take the microlight out so it doesn't get damaged, and they'll have room to run around then—or they can use the garden, if it's sunny. Hopefully it will be. Boys need room to let off steam—you could get a bouncy castle on the lawn.'

He was off again, doing things for them. 'Don't you

mind?' she asked, stunned by the way he just kept giving.

'Why should I mind? He's a good kid.'

'He set fire to my house,' she reminded him drily.

'Only by accident.'

'I know—and he won't do it again. He is a good kid, you're right. He could just do with a father's restraining hand occasionally—not that Brian ever did anything restrained. He's probably too much like him—reckless and never thinking ahead to the consequences.'

'He's just a boy,' Matt said gently. 'Boys are all the same. I shouldn't worry too much about Brian's influence—genes don't count for nearly as much as environment or example, when it comes to behaviour. Other things, yes, but being a decent human being is largely a matter of example, and he's got a good role model.'

'Thanks.' She played with her drink, touched by his words, and as if he sensed her mood he sat back and chivvied her.

'Come on, drink up or you'll be saying you don't have time to discuss menus and programmes with me.'

She drained her glass and they went back to the house via the estate office so he could pick up his car. Then they scrounged coffee off Mrs Hodges, took it up to the drawing room and toyed around with his weekend plans, until finally he put his mug down, leant over and kissed her.

'What was that for?' she said with a smile.

'Just because I haven't done it yet today, and that seemed like an oversight.' He looked at his watch. 'How long can you spare?'

She smiled again. 'Long enough.'

They stood up, leaving the plans for the weekend scattered on the table, and went into his room. The earlier irritation she'd felt with him was gone, ironed out by his straighforward reaction, and besides, she couldn't resist the need to be with him.

He closed the curtains, cutting out the light and shielding them from prying eyes, and then slowly, lazily, he removed her clothes. She waited impatiently, tolerating his slow pace because somehow it seemed to build the suspense far more than anything else.

'Your turn,' she said, and gave him the same treatment.

He groaned as her fingers brushed the taut muscles of his abdomen, then bit his lip as she slowly peeled his jeans away from his legs.

'Tease,' he murmured as she brushed against him, and drawing her into his arms, he kissed her. She moved and he laughed softly. 'You, lady, are asking for trouble,' he warned.

'Mmm.' She moved again, and fire leapt between them.

'That does it,' he laughed, his eyes ablaze. 'That's it!'

'Good,' she said with a chuckle. 'Finally!'

With a muffled groan he lifted her and laid her in the middle of the big, high bed. His mouth found hers again, and the gentle humour left them, driven out by the need they'd generated in its place.

It was much, much later before they went back to their respective duties—so much later that she was almost late to fetch the children from school. If they hadn't been distracted in the shower, of course, she thought as she ran down the lane towards the school, she would have had plenty of time and been able to park much closer. Ah, well, the exercise was no doubt good for her.

The children came out of school bubbling with excitement, because Jenny had sent an invitation to go round for tea. 'Please can we? We can see how the house is,' Joe said.

Jenny stood there and lifted her shoulders. 'Only if you've got time. I seem to have seen so little of you.'

'Sure,' she said, wondering how late she'd have to stay up to make up for spending the afternoon in bed with Matt and now this. Oh, well. Jenny was right, she hadn't seen them for ages, and she did want to see how the house was coming on.

'Lovely. Thanks. We'll follow you back.'

'Yeay!' Joe yelled, and he and Jenny's boy Tom went flying up the road to Jenny's car, diving into the back.

'I'll take Joe, shall I?' Jenny said with a wry smile.

'Sure. Whatever. Can I pick anything up at the village shop?'

Jenny shook her head. 'It's all done—I had a baking fit last night, just in case.'

The house looked better, Georgia thought, with the roof on and the soot cleaned from the windows and the brickwork.

The garden, though, was another matter. It had been trampled on the night of the fire, and she shook her head sadly over the mangled wreckage.

'It'll grow back. You just have to cut it down and accept that it won't be anything much this year. It's a shame, but at least you're all OK.'

She nodded. 'I'll just take a quick look inside,' she said, and opening the door, she called to the builders.

'Up here,' a disembodied voice said, and she found the electrician lying on the floor threading cable through the new joists.

'How's it going?' she asked, looking round at the scene of devastation. It looked like a building site, except that most building sites didn't have smoke streaks on the walls.

'OK. Only another three weeks or so and you should be back in. It's just decorating and carpets once the plasterer's been, and he can come in once the wiring's all replaced.'

She picked her way carefully over the loose boards and went back downstairs. Nothing much had changed except that they'd stripped everything out. Still, at least the insurance company had been happy to give her the go-ahead. She'd needed new carpets and curtains, and the suite was to be replaced as well, because the cleaners couldn't get the smell out of it.

It was going to be like a new house, she thought, and felt a pang of sadness that they'd have to leave Heveling to come back.

She found she didn't want to, that she wanted nothing more than to spend the rest of her life there as Matt's wife.

Still, he hadn't asked her, and she'd probably say no even if he did, just because of the money. She didn't think she'd ever be able to trust it again because of Brian—even if Matt was, as he kept pointing out, nothing like him.

She went back to Jenny's house, chatted happily with her friend while the children ate and ran around the garden in fits and starts, and then finally took her two home, tired but happy.

And then, at nearly nine o'clock, she took out the Chelsea drawings, found her books on costings and tried to work out some sort of figure for Matt, excluding the cost of the hard landscaping and the summer house.

It was past one when she went to bed, and only the sound of the microlight starting up woke her at eight.

She chivvied the children out of bed and through the
bathroom, gave them a sandwich to eat on the way and
money for school lunch, and vowed never to let Matt
distract her again!

It wasn't a problem in the next week and a half, because
they were both too busy. Georgia was drawing up plans
to submit to the Chelsea panel for approval of the new
garden design, and Matt was planning his weekend.

Joe's birthday dawned bright and clear, as it always
seemed to be for his birthday, and they had a special
breakfast of chocolate-filled croissants before Georgia
ran them to school.

As she came home, she ran into Matt—almost literally—coming out of the studio as she turned into the
courtyard.

He opened her door and leaned on it, looking lean and
sexy and fascinating to her starved senses. She'd missed
him. 'There you are,' he said. 'I've got a birthday card
for Joe. I just missed you. I wanted to know what he'd
like.'

She shrugged. 'Who knows? I have no idea how boys'
minds work. I gave him a computer game, against my
better judgement. I'll leave it up to you—why don't you
ask him tonight?'

'OK.'

'In fact,' she said, forgetting her vow to keep Matt
and the children apart, 'why don't you come for tea?
We're having a cake—if I get round to making one—
and sandwiches. About four thirty?'

'Done. I've got all the arrangements for the weekend
under way. We could do with discussing them.'

She grinned. 'I seem to remember we got distracted
last time we discussed them.'

That tantalising, crooked smile danced fleetingly over his lips. 'I don't know what you mean.'

'Liar. What time?'

'Over lunch? Even you have to eat.'

'Just lunch—and just planning the weekend. I really don't have time for anything else if I've got to make the cake.'

'I'll help you with the tea. I can make sandwiches. In fact I'll come to you at lunchtime and we can sort the tea out while we talk about the weekend.'

And of course, they were side-tracked. Still, the cake was made, in the shape of a plane because that was all Joe could talk about at the moment, and they threw together a few sandwiches before she had to go off and pick the children up.

When she got back, Matt had carried all the food out into the garden and set up a picnic under a tree, and he ruffled Joe's hair and hugged him briefly and gave him his card.

'Wow, it's a fighter plane!' he said, and zoomed round the garden, arms outstretched, making machine gun noises.

Georgia rolled her eyes and poured the drinks, then persuaded Joe to sit down long enough to eat his tea.

They had trouble with the candles on the cake, of course. Every time they were nearly all lit, one blew out. 'Can't we just pretend you're seven again?' Georgia said in mock despair.

'No!' Joe insisted. 'I want eight candles!'

So they built a windbreak with their hands, and he blew out the candles a second before the wind would have done it, and they all clapped and cheered and sang 'Happy Birthday'.

'So, young man, what do you want for your birthday?'

Matt asked him. 'I'd forgotten all about it till last night, and I didn't know what you wanted. Your mother said to ask you.'

'I want to go up in the microlight,' he said, glaring defiantly at his mother.

'Ah.'

Matt looked at Georgia, and she looked back, then shook her head. 'No. You know I won't allow it—'

'But why? You went up—if it's that dangerous, why did you go?'

Because I'm a fool for Matt, she could have said, but she didn't. 'I had to see the garden,' she said lamely instead.

'But he had photos! And anyway, it's not fair. You keep treating me like a baby, and I'm *eight* now!'

Eight. So small. So precious—

'Matt—tell her it's safe! Tell her I'll be all right! She's making such a fuss—'

'It's you that's making the fuss, and anyway, I'm your mother, I'm allowed to make a fuss.'

'Matt, please!'

Matt shook his head. 'It's your mother's decision. It's nothing to do with me, Joe, I'm not your father. You know I'm quite willing to take you up, she only has to say the word, but until she does, I'm sorry, it's no go.'

But his eyes, locked on Georgia's face, made it clear that she was being over-protective and paranoid.

'You could taxi up and down,' she compromised.

'I've already done that loads,' he said scornfully.

'Loads? When?' she asked, trying to keep the hysteria out of her voice.

'Twice, actually, and only on the grass outside the

barn,' Matt chipped in. 'We went at about twenty miles an hour.'

'I said he couldn't go in it!'

'No, you said he couldn't go *up* in it. And he didn't go up. I wouldn't defy you.' But he wanted to, she could tell. His eyes held a clear message. Let go. Let him grow up. I'll look after him.

Trust me.

Oh, help. She looked again at her son's defiant, pleading face, and wondered if she was being over-protective. Trying, perhaps, to counteract what she saw as Brian's hot-headedness. 'But Matt's busy,' she protested weakly. 'He doesn't have time.'

'Actually, he does,' Matt disagreed. 'In fact, I have to fly the microlight over to the airfield before tomorrow morning, so he could come with me—if you agreed. In fact you could follow in the car, and bring us back, which would save Simon doing it.'

'But I don't know where it is!'

'I'll show you,' he said, and disappeared out of the garden gate, coming back a few moments later with a road atlas from the car. 'Here—it's easy. You just follow the road, turn left here over the bridge, and you'll see the windsock—the orange cone thing blowing in the wind. Piece of cake.'

She closed her eyes. Eight years ago she'd struggled to give birth to him, and now Matt was going to take him up in that dangerous and hateful tool—

'It's quite safe,' he assured her quietly. 'And I will be very careful with him.'

She hesitated, still not saying yes, and obviously hesitated for long enough, because Joe leapt to his feet, hugged her and ran inside. They took the picnic remains inside, just as Joe tumbled back down the stairs in jeans and a bomber type jacket, and a baseball cap.

'Come on, then,' he said, dancing from foot to foot, and before she knew what was happening the machine was out of the barn, her baby was strapped firmly into the back and Matt was doing the pre-flight checks.

He did them twice, probably mindful of her stricken expression, she thought hysterically, and then he came over and kissed her firmly on the mouth.

'Don't panic,' he ordered gently. 'We'll see you there in a minute.'

And getting into the machine, he started the engine, taxied slowly forwards, revved up and did the last few checks and then started the take-off run.

'Oh, Lord,' she said, her hand over her mouth, and Lucy tugged her arm.

'He'th all right, Mummy, really,' she said, smiling reassuringly. 'Don't be thcared.'

'Scared?' She gave a tight little laugh. She was terrified. Scared didn't even scratch the surface! 'Come on, let's go,' she said grimly, and climbed into the car.

The map was open beside her, but she didn't need it. One eye was on the road, the other on the little blip in the sky ahead of them, and after a few moments it dipped out of sight. After another half mile or so she saw the windsock, and turned onto the runway just as the microlight taxied down towards them.

Joe was beaming in the back of it, waving to her like a windmill, and Matt signalled for her to follow them as he taxied over to the hangar and came to rest.

Her legs were nearly as weak and wobbly as when she'd been in it herself, and she had to lean on the car for support for a moment.

Matt climbed out of the microlight, grinning, and

helped Joe out of the impossibly awkward rear cockpit. He came out beaming, his eyes lit up, and rushed over to her, hugging her.

'Oh, Mum, it was excellent!' he said. 'He let me fly it!'

Her hand flew up to her mouth, and Matt winked. 'I had my hands firmly on the controls,' he assured her.

'Still, I flew it,' Joe crowed, bouncing round like a puppy, unable to contain his excitement. 'It was so cool!'

'I want to go,' Lucy said suddenly, and Georgia's heart, just settling down again, roared off into overdrive.

'No!' she said, just as Matt agreed.

'Oh, Mummy, pleathe! Joe went—it'th not fair!'

'It's his birthday,' she said.

'I don't mind,' Joe said. 'Matt says he'll take me up again. Lucy can go.'

And so, without a word being said, Matt arched a brow, took her sigh for acquiescence and hijacked her daughter.

'Matt—' she protested, but he just smiled at her.

'It's all right, Georgia. I'll be very careful.'

'She gets car sick.'

'I'll take her very gently up and round and down. Nothing fancy.'

'That's what you said to me.'

'Don't worry. I'll only go slowly, and I'll do everything very carefully and tell her first. She'll be fine.'

She wasn't, in fact. She was a little green when they landed, and a few minutes later she was sick, but at least she was alive and wasn't about to ask again.

Georgia took them home, parked them in front of the television and told them she was going to look at Matt's garden.

She was—with a fork! She was so mad with him for taking Lucy up without her express permission that if he'd come into range she would have stuck the fork through his chest.

She hoiked out one of the dead roses, then another, and finally caught her arm on a briar and ripped the skin.

'Damn,' she said, and throwing down the fork, she burst into tears.

'Silly girl,' Matt said softly from behind her, and turned her into his arms.

'Let me go, I hate you!' she yelled, pounding on his chest, but he just caught her hands in one of his and held her gently, and after a moment she sagged against him and wept.

Then, when she got her spine back, she straightened and whirled away from him, gratified to see blood all over his shirt from her slashed arm. 'You had no right to take Lucy up!' she raged. 'I didn't say you could.'

'Georgia, you have to treat them both the same, you know that—'

'Yes, I do. You don't—you don't have to treat them at all! It's nothing to do with you how I bring up my children, what I let them do or not, how fairly or unfairly I do anything! Just because you like stupid toys doesn't mean my children have to play with them!'

She ran out of air, and stood gasping, glowering at him as he stood watching her. After a long moment he closed his eyes and dragged his hand wearily over his face.

'I'm sorry,' he said. 'I thought if you were OK about Joe, you'd be OK about Lucy. Obviously I was wrong.'

'I wasn't OK about Joe—I wasn't OK at all, but it's his birthday, and you all made me feel fussy and over-protective, and I was terrified the whole time!'

'It's all part of love, isn't it—being scared for your children and your loved ones when they do things that have an element of risk? It's because you're a good mother. You worry—but you have to start letting go, Georgia,' he said gently. 'They're weaned now. They can walk unaided. That means they can do things without you. You have to learn to let go a little, so they can learn how to cope independently. It's tough, but it's true.'

He was right, of course, but that didn't mean she had to like it.

She looked down at her arm, and his eyes tracked to it and back to her face.

'That needs cleaning up. Come into the kitchen, I'll do it. I've got a first-aid kit in there.'

She followed him, letting him wash and dry the nasty scratch, and sitting in grim-lipped silence while he pulled out the broken thorns embedded in her arm. Then he dressed it, pulled her to her feet and kissed her, and with a sigh she let him hold her against his chest.

'I just feel so alone all the time, and because I am, I can't let anybody else make any decisions for them. I'm sorry I shouted.'

'That's OK. I'm sorry I took Lucy up without your permission. Can we be friends again?'

His eyes were so sincere. She felt the last trace of her anger drain away.

'OK,' she said with a tired smile.

'Good.'

He kissed her again, then sent her back to her children.

'Are you cross, Mum?' Joe said anxiously as she went in.

She shook her head. 'No, darling.'

'You've hurt your arm—what happened?' Lucy asked, eyes wide.

'A rose got me. It's all right. Matt's dealt with it.'

And she thought that Matt seemed to be dealing with an awful lot these days, and she wondered exactly where it was leading them all.

If anywhere.

CHAPTER NINE

THE guests arrived promptly at ten the next morning, by which time Georgia had dropped the children with Jenny, cut armloads of flowers from her abandoned garden and brought them back and arranged them in simple vases around the hall and the downstairs drawing room which the guests would use.

She'd also gone out to the walled garden and tidied up the roses she'd been digging out the night before, then gone back to the coach house and changed into a new skirt and blouse, the only things other than jeans and the Chelsea dress that she possessed at the moment!

At ten to ten, just as she'd been coming out of her bedroom, there had been a tap on the door. She'd opened it to Matt, looking as gorgeous as ever in casual slacks and an open-necked shirt, one hand propped high on the doorframe.

'All ready?' he asked, looking her over.

'Yes—will I do? It's this or the Chelsea dress, and I was going to wear that tonight.'

He smiled and kissed her—on the cheek, in deference to her lipstick?—and reassured her. 'You're fine like that. You look lovely. How's your arm?'

'Oh.' She looked down at it and wrinkled her nose. 'Sore. It's my own fault, I shouldn't have lost my temper.'

'You were provoked. The flowers in the house look lovely, by the way. Are they from your garden?'

'Yes. I didn't like to cut yours because the ladies may

well want to stroll round, and my garden's going to waste at the moment. I nicked some greenery, though.'

They walked slowly towards the house, scanning the drive for any cars. 'At least it's a nice day,' Matt said. 'If it's pouring with rain, or foggy, it's not nearly so easy or safe to fly.'

'Is it ever safe to fly?' she asked with a shudder.

'Of course—ah, here we are. Our first guests.'

It was interesting to watch him in action, she thought. Interesting and a bit unnerving. She'd got used to him being the easygoing, genial land-owner pottering about the countryside in his Discovery, chatting to the farm manager, or Mr Hodges who did the maintenance on the estate.

To see him as the equally easygoing and genial but very slick host was a bit odd.

By ten-thirty everyone had arrived, and he'd introduced her simply as Georgia Beckett—'a friend of mine'. Friend? she thought. Still, lover was a bit much, and partner probably implied more than they had.

But friend? Somehow that hurt.

He took the men off, and she was left with the women—four of them, varying in age from thirty-odd to sixty, and as different as chalk and cheese. Keeping them off each other's throats and happy for the rest of the day was probably going to be a challenge, she thought with grim humour.

'Do you fly?' one of the women asked as they sipped another cup of coffee after the men left.

'Me?' she said with a mock shudder. 'Oh, no. I've been up once—never again!'

'I hate it,' the middle-aged woman dripping with ostentatious jewellery said. 'I always think it's not natural, but there's no telling Barry. He's quite determined!'

'We fly a lot,' the youngest woman said. 'We've got a light plane we use for his business, but John wants something a little smaller just for fun—a bit more grass roots, he says. He's a real enthusiast. He wants to build it himself.'

'Oh, I couldn't trust that,' Mrs Drippy-Jewels said with a shudder that shook her jowls. 'If Barry had screwed it together, I'd be sure it'd fall down out of the sky just as surely as his shelves used to come off the walls!'

They all laughed, and the quiet, mousy woman asked Georgia if she thought they were safe.

'Oh. I just hate them so much I can't get past it, but yes, they are safe.' She was surprised at the confidence with which she said it, and she realised with astonishment that she actually believed it!

'Would you let your children go in one?' Mrs Drippy-Jewels asked. 'That's the acid test.'

Georgia laughed. 'Well, funnily enough I did, only last night. It was my son's birthday, and that was what he wanted for a present, so I gave in and let Matt take him up. He loved it. My daughter was sick afterwards, but even she seemed to enjoy it.'

She didn't mention the tantrum she'd thrown, or Matt's apology. It wasn't in her interests to scupper the company before Chelsea!

'I'd like to see the factory.'

Georgia looked at the speaker, a silver-haired woman in her sixties, elegant and very self-contained. Mrs Greaves?

'So would I.' That was the young woman, the one who had the light plane already.

The other two agreed, and so Georgia lifted her shoulders in a Gallic shrug and smiled. 'You know what? So would I—shall I ring?'

They smiled back.

'Do,' Mrs Greaves said. 'I don't see why they should have all the fun.'

So Georgia rang, and after a second or so of stunned silence, Matt laughed. 'OK. Bring them up. It can't hurt.' He gave her quick directions, then added, 'Use the Mercedes—or are you going to tell me you can't drive an automatic?'

'I wouldn't dream of it. It means one less thing to think about, so I'm less likely to take the side out on a gate.'

She could almost feel him wince. 'OK. Drive carefully. We'll see you in a while.'

The ladies loved it. They poked and prodded and asked intelligent questions, examined all the various stages of wing construction from bonding the plywood cover to the Styrofoam sheets that made the ribs inside the leading edge, applying and heat-shrinking the polyester fabric, to 'doping' the wing with special aircraft sealant to make the fabric impervious to weather. They climbed in and out of a cockpit, tapped and waggled the flaps, and then wanted to fly.

Well, some of them! The lady with the jewellery didn't, predictably, and the other middle-aged one who so far had said very little didn't want to either, but they both wanted to watch, and so they set off in convoy to the airfield.

Hours later they returned to the house for a late lunch, full of enthusiasm for the little planes. Even though they were such very different people, the trip to the factory and airfield seemed to have given them something in common, and the barriers tumbled down and they all relaxed.

Lunch was a noisy and casual affair as a result, and Georgia decided it was a good job Matt wasn't paying her, because she wasn't working hard enough to earn it!

Then after coffee the men disappeared again, and Georgia took the ladies, at their request, on a guided tour of the gardens.

'What delightful roses!' Mrs Greaves exclaimed as they went into the walled garden.

'They will be,' Georgia said wryly. 'Most of them are original, I think—there's a *Red Book* for this part of the garden which lists them—'

'Really? A *Red Book*? Oh, my dear, how exciting!' Mrs Greaves said with an awed expression. 'May I see it?'

'Of course—it shows the formal parterre which we're restoring—that's why the turf's all cut off and there are lines drawn all over the soil. We've got to plant the little hedges next, and the perennials in the centre of each, but I feel a bit of a fraud because all the plans are drawn up and I only have to make sure everything goes in the right place!'

'And do you know about these things? Are you an expert?' Mrs Greaves asked, bending to smell a rose.

'Well, I don't know about an expert, but I am a garden designer.'

Mrs Greaves straightened and looked at her. 'Georgia Beckett—of course! My dear, I thought I'd heard of you. You did a garden for a friend of mine in London—oh, must be five years ago! Claudia Raymond. It won an award.'

Georgia smiled and coloured. 'That's right. It was a lovely design brief. I really enjoyed her garden.'

'My dear, you should see it now! Wonderful.

Everything's matured beautifully. I shall so enjoy telling her I've seen you.' She took Georgia's arm and strolled on round the roses. 'So, tell me, Georgia, what have you been doing with yourself since then?'

'Well, designing all sorts of things, really.'

'Any more awards?'

She laughed. 'Not like that one. I'm doing a garden at Chelsea next year, though—Matt's company is sponsoring me, and we're taking the summer house with us and rebuilding it there, with a parterre and fountain and rose border—the design isn't final yet, but it's coming on.'

'I must be sure and come and see it—I always make a point of going on the Gala night and Members' Day. So much more fun without the crowds, don't you think?'

Georgia, who had only had the privilege of enjoying it once without the crowds, had to agree.

Mrs Drippy-Jewels waved a hand from the other side of the garden. 'Do you know this funny rose has two different coloured flowers on it?' she said.

'Yes—it's a York and Lancaster rose; it's called that because it brought together the Tudor Roses of the houses of York and Lancaster on the same bush, and so brought unity and peace—or so the saying goes! That's its only claim to fame, though. It's not exactly a spectacular rose!'

They chuckled at the apt description of the rather sparse bush, and then went back inside to rustle up a cup of tea and so that Georgia could show them her preliminary sketches for Chelsea, and also the *Red Book*. Mrs Greaves had been at pains to tell them they were in the company of someone of some standing, and Georgia had to stifle the urge to gag her, and endure the praise and inquisition.

'Would you like to see the studio?' she asked, and of course they said yes, so armed with their cups of tea they set off across the courtyard to the barn.

It took Georgia ages to get them out. They seemed to be interested in everything, and the lady with the jewellery turned out to have been a graphic artist in her time, and was in fact very knowledgeable—which just goes to prove, Georgia Beckett, that you can't judge every cat by its skin, she told herself sternly.

Dinner was an even greater success than lunch, but it was a rowdy party and it didn't break up until nearly two in the morning.

When the guests had finally retired to bed, Matt walked her home and stood for a few moments just holding her in the quiet of her sitting room.

'Thank you so much for today,' he said softly. 'They all seem to have really enjoyed it.'

Georgia realised she had, too. How odd. She'd thought it would be hateful, and yet, maybe because Matt was such a good host, and maybe just because he was appreciative, she'd managed to have fun.

And she'd felt part of it all, which in reality she wasn't.

'It's been a pleasure,' she told him with honesty.

He hugged her gently, then gave her a tender, lingering kiss before releasing her with obvious reluctance.

'I have to go back to them,' he said. 'They might be wandering around trying to find things and getting lost. I'll see you in the morning.'

'I'll come and say goodbye before they go,' she promised, and kissed him again.

It seemed odd to shut the door behind him. After an evening like that, they should have gone up to bed together. It was where they belonged, she thought—but perhaps he didn't? Maybe he felt that this was close enough—accessible when passion was running high, but not too much of an inconvenience when it wasn't.

And maybe it was just a question of propriety in front of his guests, and not wishing to compromise her? Outdated, surely, in this day and age, but possibly not to Mrs Greaves.

Oh, damn. If only she could come right out with it and ask him!

'It's been such a pleasure to meet you, my dear—just wait till I tell Claudia that you're going to Chelsea! She'll be so thrilled!'

'Do give her my regards, won't you? I'd love a photo of the garden, as well, if possible. I ought to give you my address—'

Mrs Greaves laughed. 'That's all right, dear. We have it.'

She got into the car beside her husband before Georgia could correct her, waved cheerfully to them and cruised slowly down the drive.

They watched the car until it crossed the bridge and turned onto the lane, then Matt looked at Georgia and grinned. 'Brilliant. Four happy couples, lots of publicity—and maybe some sales.'

'I think John and Angela want one, don't they? A kit?'

'Yes—and Mr Greaves. I'm not sure about the others, but possibly. I think the wives are less keen. It was a master stroke bringing the women up to the factory. I'd never have thought of it, but I suppose if there's that much going out of the family coffers, everyone takes an interest!'

Unless the coffers were so deep it didn't matter. 'I think it was more concern for safety and interest in the construction methods, to be honest. Women do fret about such things.'

Matt laughed, his eyes crinkling at the corners. 'You don't say?' he teased. Then he slipped his hand into his pocket and pulled out a long, slim box and handed it to her.

'Here—with my love.'

She eyed the box suspiciously. 'What's that?'

'Just a little thank-you for everything you've done over the weekend.'

She didn't want a thank-you. She wanted much more. She wanted to have been part of it, to have been involved in the planning and choice of dates, the guest list, the accommodation—she wanted, she realised in shock, to be his wife.

Numb with that realisation, she took the box and opened it. Inside, nestled in white satin, was a fine gold pen, the sort used for drawing and graphics, stunningly high quality and engraved with her name.

Her eyes prickled with tears. She'd thought it would be a watch or necklace or something tacky like that, but it wasn't. It was a lovely gift, truly useful to her, but for all that it wasn't what she wanted. She couldn't tell him that, though, not while he was standing there looking hopeful but a trifle uncertain, as he was.

'It's lovely,' she said honestly. 'Thank you. You didn't need to do this.'

'I know. You would have done it all for love.' He gave her a wry grin, and she wondered if he had any idea how close to the truth he'd come.

She looked away, the prickle of tears growing more insistent, and took a steadying breath.

'So, what now?' he said.

'I fetch the children, do Mummy things with them for

the rest of the morning and then this afternoon it's Joe's party—we're off to Roller Magic for burgers and buns and broken ankles.'

He laughed. 'You're mad. Want a hand with them all?'

'I expect you're busy,' she said, trying to dissuade him, but he wouldn't be put off. Damn. Now she was going to have him there with her all afternoon, doing Man Stuff with the boys and giving her heart grief.

Just what she needed!

He was brilliant with the boys. Georgia, who couldn't rollerskate to save her life, sat on the side with a cup of coffee and watched him in awe as he whizzed round, dodging through the kids, leading strings of them all connected together like a centipede on wheels, then teaching them how to turn and go backwards, how to jump, how to spin—

How did he know all that? The boys were hugely impressed, of course, and disappointed when he shook his head and skated slowly over to her, collapsing on the other chair totally out of breath. Beads of sweat glistened on his forehead, and he wiped his face on his shoulder and grinned.

'That is more fun than I've had in years,' he said with a laugh.

'You're good,' she conceded, knowing it would inflate his ego.

It didn't. He shook his head. 'Not like I used to be. I used to skate a lot—nothing fancy, just fast enough to impress the girls, you know the sort of thing.'

She did. It still worked, but she wasn't telling him that!

He stretched out his jeans-clad legs, locked his hands

behind his head and watched the children. Georgia watched him. He was just too decorative to miss!

Other women were watching him, too, which gave her a proprietorial sort of pride, until she remembered she'd got no right to feel like that.

'Coffee?' she said, standing up abruptly.

'Something cold—I'll get it.'

And he stood up and skated over to the counter, Georgia following at a more sedate pace. The girl serving there flirted with him, and Georgia wanted to scratch her eyes out.

It shocked her.

'When do you want to give them tea?' the girl asked Matt, and he turned to Georgia.

'What time?'

The girl blinked, as if she'd only just noticed Georgia's insignificant presence.

'Soon, I think, if possible?' she said sweetly.

'Twenty minutes?'

'Fine.'

She smiled at Matt again, her lashes drooping seductively, and as they went back to the table with their drinks he chuckled.

'I thought I was getting too old for those sort of looks,' he murmured.

'It's because you've been behaving like a teenager,' she said nastily.

'Ooo-ee,' he said in a sing-song voice. 'Are we a touch put out?'

'Do you realise how much I'm going to have to listen to this?' she said, pretending to be cross. 'Matt did this—Matt did that—Matt can do so-and-so! Joe is going to be a grade A pain about it—and it's all your fault, you show-off!'

She laughed. She couldn't help it. She tried so hard to keep a straight face, but he rolled his eyes and chuckled and undermined her self-control. She didn't care. He'd been great with the kids, and they'd all had more fun as a result of him being there.

A delegation came a few moments later and towed him off for more games, and she sipped her coffee and watched him and knew exactly how the waitress felt!

The rose garden made slow but steady progress. Over the next few days she cleared out the rest of the redundant bushes with the help of Mr Hodges, and then they planted the little lines of box that would form the structure of the formal parterre.

It was a dreadful time of year to plant, of course, but every evening the hedges were watered copiously, and they soon settled in and started to grow in the warm sunshine.

From the old drawing room upstairs it was possible to see the design taking shape, and Georgia would go and sit there sometimes and contemplate the garden, seeing it full of colour and texture and with the formal structure of the little clipped hedges to give it all a certain tension.

Would she still be here when it was mature? Or would it be like Claudia Raymond's garden, that she would hear about from others but never see again?

That thought was so acutely painful she dismissed it. She'd put so much of herself into Matt's garden—not in terms of design, of course, because of Repton's wonderful record of it all, but in terms of emotion, care in the planting, the choice of the little bushes, the trimming and tidying of the roses, the hands-on aspects that she never usually did but passed on to someone else.

The idea that this garden would be looked down on and enjoyed by Matt with another woman at his side was devastating, but she had to be realistic. If she wasn't around—and she began to realise that she wouldn't be, not under her terms—then someone else would be, someone less worried about the permanence of the relationship, someone who would take what was on offer graciously and not plague herself with might-have-beens.

She found herself avoiding Matt, too, making excuses not to make love. Beautiful though his lovemaking was, it wasn't enough, and she knew he wasn't in the market for more.

And then the builders told her that her house was ready. She went and checked it over, and wondered what she'd ever seen in it.

Security, of course, and sensible accommodation that she could maintain herself—all very laudable reasons for buying it, but not exciting. Nothing about it made her heart glad. Nothing made her sigh with contentment.

Except the garden, of course, which was her pride and joy. Jenny had kindly been watering it for her, and so it didn't look as bad as it could have done.

She went out into it and looked around, and it seemed small and cramped. She was used to the scale of Heveling now, and she wondered how she would learn to squeeze them all back into such a little house and garden.

She went back into the house and looked around again. All trace of the fire was gone, even the lingering smell of smoke, overlaid now by the pungent fumes of fresh paint.

All she had to do was phone up the carpet firm, have them fit the new carpets throughout the upstairs and the hall and landing, have the new furniture sent round and then they could move back in.

A huge lump rose in her throat. She didn't want to leave Matt, but she knew it couldn't go on. She'd just have to be tough. She'd known what she was doing, after all. She'd gone into it with her eyes open, and it had been her that had pushed their relationship on to the next stage.

And now, she thought wretchedly, she'd reap the consequences.

'Do you have to go?'

They were standing in the drawing room, looking down over the walled garden. The little hedges were growing, the centres had been planted, the fountain was installed in the middle of the maze, and the roses round the edge were looking much happier for their tidy-up.

'Yes,' she said emptily. 'I have to.'

'I'll miss having you around the place. I've got used to driving past the studio and waving to you. It'll be odd not having you all here.'

Not odd without her in his life, please note, she thought sadly.

'The house is ready. It's silly to stay here.' She turned to him. 'You've been so kind. I can't thank you enough for all you've done.'

'Come to bed,' he said softly. 'I just want to hold you—touch you. It's been so long.'

She swallowed. She ached for him. She couldn't walk away.

'Please?' he added, his voice gruff.

She nodded wordlessly, and he put his arm round her and led her to his room. The curtains were open, but he left them. There was no-one about to see them, and they had other things to think about.

For the first time their lovemaking wasn't slow and tender. As if their bodies knew it was the last time, they clung together with a feverish desperation, and when it was over Georgia couldn't stop the tears. They slithered into her hair and dripped in her ears, and she scrubbed them away angrily.

'Oh, Georgia,' he murmured, and kissed them away, and then the next wave, and the next, until finally she buried her head in his chest and wept.

'Darling, what's wrong?' he asked tenderly.

She sat up, pulling the bedclothes round her, dragging in much needed air.

'I have to go,' she said tearfully.

'You're not just talking about the house, are you?' he said slowly. As if in self-defence, he pulled on his jeans and sat beside her. 'What's brought this on, Georgia?'

She dragged in more air. 'Nothing. I just love it here. I don't want to move.'

'So stay. You don't have to go. You're welcome here, you know that. I don't want you to go.'

Tell me you love me! Ask me to marry you! she nearly screamed, but he didn't.

And that was the problem. She needed to be independent, but perversely, she still needed to be needed—and Matt didn't need her. He wanted her, he liked her company, he enjoyed her in bed—but he didn't need her in his life, and he didn't love her.

Wordlessly, she pulled on her clothes, dragged her hair back into a scrunchie and went down to the kitchen and out across the yard. Their possessions—clothes and so forth—were in her car, everything else had already been delivered and installed. She took one last look around the coach house, and was just coming out when Murphy padded in and laid his great head against her side.

'Oh, Murphy, I'll miss you,' she said, and nearly started to cry again.

'We'll both miss you all,' Matt said.

He was standing by the porch, no laughter in his eyes for once, and she thought his throat worked just a little.

'I'd better go—I've got to unpack this lot before I fetch the children from school. Goodbye, Matt—and thanks again for everything.'

'My pleasure,' he said gruffly. For an age he hesitated, then taking her in his arms, he kissed her.

It was like the last kiss of a condemned man, she thought, dazed, as he released her abruptly and turned away.

'Murphy, come.'

He strode off, out across the park, with Murphy bounding along beside him, and Georgia watched him until his figure blurred.

'Damn you,' she said softly, blinking the tears away, and getting into her car she went slowly down the drive for the last time, turned left over the bridge and headed for Henfield, her heart in tatters.

CHAPTER TEN

IT WAS odd in the house, with so much of it new and so many of their things replaced. It was almost as if they'd stepped into someone else's lives—and although the children settled back quite quickly, Georgia found herself staring out of her window at the stars night after night, and longing for Matt.

She had a letter from him a few days after they moved back in, enclosing another letter with a London postmark and telling her that three of the four couples who'd stayed had ordered microlights. Murphy, it transpired, was going to be a father, to the considerable annoyance of the bitch's owner, and would she like a wolfhound/Newfoundland cross puppy in due course?

The thought of such a huge and ungainly dog in her tiny house reduced her to tears of laughter—tears that quickly changed to tears of regret that she wouldn't see the puppies.

Because she wouldn't, of course. She would stay firmly away from Matt, and let Terry and Mick go and survey the summer house and do the detailed technical drawings of the structure for the Chelsea design.

The knot garden was finished; all that remained was planting the roses in the gaps in the border come autumn, and Mr Hodges could do that.

No, she didn't need to go back again. She put his letter down, resisting the urge to hold it to her heart like a Victorian virgin with the vapours, and slit open the other envelope.

Photos fell out, of wonderful colourful shrubs and perennials, all tangled together in exotic profusion. The
hard landscaping was softened by the mature plants, the
whole thing mellowed down and absolutely as she would
have wanted it.

Claudia Raymond was obviously taking good care of
her garden.

She took the letter out, and scanned it, then read it
again word for word.

My dear Georgia,
It was a delight to meet you. Henry and I have been
talking, and we wondered if you would be kind
enough to redesign our London garden. Of course it's
nothing like as grand as the lovely garden you and
Matt have, but we do spend a great deal of time in it,
and we'd be so grateful if you'd at least come and
talk to us about what we might do with it. My tele-
phone number is at the top—do ring and talk to me
when you've received this.
Yours, Gillian Greaves

She put the letter down and laughed softly. So much
for shocking Mrs Greaves with their relationship—it
seemed she'd taken it for granted!

She rang the number immediately, and arranged to
visit her the following day. She didn't really have time
to take on anything else, but if she wasn't sleeping at
night, she might as well be doing something useful—
and anyway, she liked Gillian Greaves and thought she'd
take care of her garden.

She went on the early train, leaving Jenny to take her
children to school and pick them up at the end of the

day, and arrived at the house in Swiss Cottage just after ten.

Mrs Greaves welcomed her with her usual charm, and ushered her into a lovely house full of antiques and fascinating little knick-knacks that must have been worth a fortune. 'Let's make coffee and take it in the garden—Henry's out for the day, so we've got the place to ourselves. Luxury!'

Georgia laughed with her hostess, but couldn't agree. She was sick of having her place to herself, and longed to have Matt to share it with. In Gillian Greaves' position, she would be lapping up every moment of Henry's company!

'Well, here it is,' she said, pushing open the back door and leading Georgia out into a small walled garden. 'I'm afraid it's only tiny, and there's not a great deal we can do about that, but it does get a lot of sun and it's so nice to sit outside amongst the birds and the flowers, don't you think?'

'Absolutely.' Georgia listened, and was amazed at how quiet and tranquil it was compared to the bustle of the huge sprawling city just outside the front door. 'It's very peaceful,' she commented.

'Oh, yes—and that's what we want, of course. We live in the country when we can, but because Henry's work is in London we're here more than the Surrey house. Pity, but there you are. Anyway, my dear, cream?'

She passed Georgia a cup of fragrant, freshly brewed coffee with smooth, silky cream on top, and Georgia sipped it and looked around, taking in the existing hard landscaping, the features that couldn't change, and things that really ought to remain.

'The only thing Henry said was, could you please leave the tree?'

'Absolutely,' Georgia agreed. 'It's at the top of my list of things to stay! So, what do you want? Colour? Scent? Cottage garden, architectural, structured, geometric, ultra-modern? Tell me how you see it.'

And she did, because she was a sensible, well-thought out person, and she'd given the matter consideration in advance.

Georgia made notes, took lots of photos, played around with a few random ideas and sketches, and ate the most superb lunch which her hostess had prepared while she'd been fiddling.

'What do you think?' she asked as they washed down their fruit compôte with sips of fragrant jasmine tea.

Gillian Greaves shuffled through the sketches, dismissing one or two, pulling out features she liked in others, and then turned to the last one. 'Oh, yes. Oh, I love the water feature—that is water, isn't it? Yes, I think water would be lovely, and of course it would help drown out the background roar of the traffic.' She chuckled, passed the sketches back to Georgia and smiled. 'I think we're going to be able to come up with something very beautiful between us, don't you? I'm really excited. I'm so glad I met you.'

The doorbell pealed in the distance, and she jumped up. 'Oh, good, she's in time. Stay there.'

Georgia, puzzled, did as she was told, and moments later Claudia Raymond came out into the garden and hugged her. 'Georgia, dear—how are you? Did you get the photographs?'

'Yes, I did—thanks. You're taking really good care of it.'

'Oh, no, it takes care of itself. It's such an easy garden

I can't tell you. So, tell me what you're doing now—I know your husband died. I was sorry to hear that.'

She shrugged. 'It was a long time ago.'

'He didn't like you working, did he?'

'No,' she agreed, marvelling at the understatement. 'Anyway, after he died I moved to Suffolk, and carried on. That's all, really. I'd already made a reputation, I had a few friends up that way by coincidence, and my brother was nearby—it seemed sensible. I took another course at a horticultural college in my free time, and just carried on.'

'And the children? Two, wasn't it?'

'Yes—a boy and a girl. They're fine, thank you.'

'And Gillian tells me there's a wonderful man in your life, in a fabulous house,' she said with a knowing smile.

Georgia faltered. 'Um—well, not really. I don't actually live there.'

Gillian Greaves gasped and put her hand over her mouth in horror. 'Oh, but I thought you did! Oh, my dear, I am so sorry, but I thought—the way he looked at you—I do beg your pardon.'

Georgia gave a strained smile. 'No, you're quite right. There was something between us—and I was living there, in the coach house. I've moved out, though. I had a house fire, and I was there while it was repaired. That was all.'

'And you and Matt?'

She shook her head. 'It's all dwindled to a halt, really. Pity, but there you are. You can't have everything you want.'

'Oh, Georgia, I am so sorry. And I know just how much you loved that garden. Oh, well, things move on, I suppose. I'm sure there'll be another man before long—they must be beating a path to your door. You're such a pretty girl, and with so much talent.'

Not that it cut any ice with Matt. Or perhaps it was just her prettiness and talent that he was interested in, and not her welfare and emotional happiness.

She finished her tea, confirmed the sort of garden they were working towards, said goodbye to her hostess and Mrs Raymond and escaped without making a complete fool of herself and bursting into tears.

She gave the poor, unsuspecting taxi driver the benefit of that experience instead.

'Hi.'

Georgia's heart smashed against her ribs and came to a grinding halt. 'Hi yourself,' she managed. She hung onto the door, unable to let go in case she fell over. Matt was leaning against her door frame, one hand high over her head, the other shoved deep into his trouser pocket. He looked tired and drawn, and he wasn't smiling.

'May I come in?'

She hesitated, then took him into the kitchen. The children were still at school, and Terry and Sal were working in the studio. She could hear them bickering in the background, resenting the lack of space after the barn.

She could understand that. It was pretty crowded in the kitchen, too.

'So, what can I do for you?' she asked with an over-bright smile.

'Talk to me? Come and visit me—let me take you out? You're avoiding me. I want to know why. I want to know what I've done.'

Or what you haven't done, Georgia thought.

'Nothing at all,' she said truthfully.

'And yet you won't return my calls or my letters.'

'I was going to.'

'When? After Chelsea?'

That's what he wants, she thought. He wants to make sure it's all going smoothly, to protect his investment. Her heart plummeted.

'Don't worry, it's all happening according to plan. The design's been approved in principle, and I've ordered the plants—or were you going to tell me you've changed your mind?'

'I wouldn't do that. You know I wouldn't—I gave you my word.'

He had. She felt a prickle of guilt in amongst the wildly tumbling emotions she was experiencing at his nearness. 'Sorry. Anyway, the builder's going to contact you to come and look at the summer house.'

'And you'll be there.'

'I don't really need to be there—'

'Oh, I think you do, Georgia. I don't think you can bottle out at this point. Clearly you've decided that whatever was between us is over, but I'm not letting you get out of your commitment to Chelsea. I'm putting a lot of money into it, and I expect to get my return. Is that clear?'

'As crystal,' she said tightly. 'And now, if you'll excuse me, I have to fetch my children from school.'

She walked past him, opened the door and held it until he went out, then shut it with a defiant little bang.

'Damn.'

She sat down on the bottom step, dropped her head onto her knees and howled her eyes out.

'Georgia? My God, what's happened? Who was that?'

She pushed Sal aside, scrubbing at her nose with a

mangled tissue and shaking her head. 'Nothing. It was Matt. It's nothing—just me.'

'Oh, hell.' Sal plopped down on the step beside her, shoved her bottom across a bit to make more room and looked up at Terry, who was hovering uncertainly in the hall.

'Terry, put the kettle on and make yourself scarce—fetch the children for her, and take them for a burger. This is girl-talk. Now, what on earth is going on? One minute you're all over each other, the next you've moved out back here and you aren't seeing him again and you look like something the cat's dragged in! What's happening, Georgia?'

'I love him,' she said sadly, and started to cry again.

'And does he love you?'

She shook her head.

'And does he know you love him?'

She shook her head.

'So he might love you and not have told you, just like you love him and haven't told him—eh?'

'Eh, nothing. He doesn't love me—he's not the marrying kind, Sal. He's the love 'em and leave 'em kind. I should have realised that. All that money—if he was the marrying kind someone would have snared him years ago.'

'Maybe he was waiting for you.'

She laughed, a little hysterically. 'I don't think so. If he was waiting for someone, it wouldn't be a lunatic redhead with a crazy career and an arsonist for a son, would it?'

'He's not an arsonist, he's an idiot,' Sal corrected candidly, 'and anyway, why not? You're lovely, Georgia. You put yourself down all the time, but you're gorgeous. You're such a nice person—well, most of the time. You can be a bit of a dragon coming up to a deadline, but most of the time you're all right. Why wouldn't he want you?'

'I don't know. Ask him.'

'Why don't you?'

She looked at Sal in horror. 'Don't be ridiculous. It's bad enough knowing he's not interested in anything but Chelsea and what he's spending his money on, without humiliating myself to boot.'

She stood up and went into the kitchen, washing her face at the sink and blotting it dry on a teatowel. 'Tea?' she said to Sal.

'Yes, I'll make it. You put strange teabags in since you moved to Heveling—flowery stuff. Dead weird. Sit down.'

'Sal, I'm just fed up, I don't need nursing,' she protested.

'Yeah, you do. When did you last eat anything more complex than a jam sandwich?'

She couldn't remember. She took the tea—hot, strong, builders' tea, quite unlike the subtle and delicate blend Matt favoured—and sipped it gratefully. 'You're a love, Sal,' she said affectionately. 'Even if you do make awful tea. Thanks for being here.'

Sal nodded and buried her nose in her mug, embarrassed at the sentimental words. She liked to pretend she was a tough cookie, with her endlessly pierced bits of anatomy and biker jeans, but actually she was a darling, and Georgia treasured her off-hand friendship.

And so, because she treasured her, she drank the awful tea, and then pulled herself together and went into the studio and tackled the garden design for Mrs Greaves.

'Terry took us to get burgers,' Joe said, bursting in a few minutes later, 'and we got you one with large fries and a chocolate milkshake because Terry said you were getting skinny.'

She looked up from her drawing board and put the cap on her gold pen that Matt had given her.

'I'm not skinny—I'm just not fat any more,' she said, denying her loss of appetite. 'So, where is it, then?'

'In the garden—Terry said come out, and Sal too. He's got her some. Hi, Sal.'

And he rushed out again, papers fluttering to the floor in his wake.

They exchanged wry smiles, and followed him out with a little more dignity.

'Georgia?'

'Matt.' She sat down abruptly, her heart thrashing. He was the last person she'd expected to ring. 'What can I do for you?' she said, gathering her scattered wits.

'The builder's coming up tomorrow to see the summer house—he'll be here at ten. Will that be any good?'

'For what?'

'For you—to come over. I want you here, remember.'

She remembered. He wanted her—but only for the builder, and to get his money's worth. 'Ten's fine,' she agreed through gritted teeth, and wondered how she'd get through it.

She took the children to school in the morning, then went home to sort out a few details on Mrs Greaves before leaving to go to Heveling. She caught Sal stuffing bags into her car, a guilty look on her face.

'What on earth's going on?' she asked.

'Oh, thank God you're here! You won't believe what I've done! I was being really cheeky, looking through your new clothes in your wardrobe to find something to borrow—I've got to go to a posh do, and you know me,

I don't have posh—anyway, I fell over my feet and I've chucked tea all over your clothes! You know what a klutz I am!'

Georgia stared, horrified, at all the bags. Most of the replacement clothes she'd never worn, and here they were, being bundled off without ceremony.

'Do I have anything left?' she asked candidly. 'I have to meet Matt and the builder—I did think I might wear something decent to bolster my confidence, and now I discover I'm going in what I've got on!'

They both looked down at her paint-spattered jeans, and Sal clapped a hand over her face.

'There's a dress on the bed—I pulled it out to ask you, and it was when I turned round to shut the wardrobe I spilt the tea. Oh, Georgia, I'm so sorry—perhaps you can wear that dress?'

'I'll find something, don't worry. Just get that lot to the cleaners. I know your tea—it's half milk, half sugar. They'll be ruined.'

She went inside, leaving Sal grinding gears on the drive, and found her wardrobe empty except for a heavy wool coat, a winter suit and a few hangers.

And on the bed was the Chelsea dress.

How appropriate, she thought, because she'd decided to tell him she was pulling out.

She put it on, buttoning it savagely without thinking about the first time they'd made love, when he'd undone the buttons one by one and left a trail of kisses that followed his fingers faithfully...

Damn. She swiped the tears away, did up the last button, slipped her feet into cool sandals and stood back.

She was thinner. That much was obvious. The dress

hung where before she'd filled it, but it still looked good—quite apart from which it was the only thing left.

She ran downstairs, stuck her head round the studio door and told them she was going, went back to gather up all the drawings that had been done to date in case the builder hadn't brought his, and ran out to her car.

She was late. Damn. She shot along the lanes, skidded onto the drive and over the bridge, and pulled up outside the barn. The builder's car was nowhere to be seen, but Mr Hodges raised a hand to her as he got into his.

She went to the front door, ringing the bell, and heard Murphy bark in the distance. Mrs Hodges opened the door, and looked her up and down with a critical eye.

'You're looking thin,' she scolded gently. 'He's in the walled garden, and the dog's shut in the kitchen. I'm just going to the market with Mr Hodges—we'll be back late this afternoon, so you'll have to fend for yourselves, I'm afraid. Just go on through, dear, you know the way.'

And she went out of the front door, closing it behind her with a little thump, leaving Georgia in the hall.

Her heart was pounding, but she didn't hesitate. She walked down the hall to the door at the end, and out into the walled garden. She'd tell him now, before the builder came, and then it was up to him if he wanted to take her design and carry on himself.

There was no sign of him. She stood for a moment, looking at the neat little hedges and the fluffy perennials between them, and the roses round the wall, mostly over now. Not many of the old type of roses flowered beyond the end of July, and she was glad she'd seen them at their best.

She wandered round, fingers trailing over the tops of the geraniums, the droning of bees blending with the sound of the harvesters on the other side of the park.

She crossed the path to the rose border to see the few that were left. Quatre Saisons, of course, the Four Seasons rose, so called because it seemed to flower all year, was sprinkled with blossoms. She might have known it would be in flower still. She bent over, cupping one of the clear pink blooms and burying her nose in it, and the glorious fragrance seemed to envelop her.

She stood up, hugging herself, and wished Matt was here. She was tense, knowing what she had to do, and she was bitterly regretting wearing the dress. She should have put her other jeans on, the ones in the drawer. Why on earth had she let a silly accident force her into something so stupid?

Sensing something, she turned round, scanning the garden, and saw him standing in the doorway of the summer house.

'Hello, Georgia,' he said.

He wasn't wearing jeans, for a change, but casual trousers, beautifully cut and doing wonderful things for his physique. Not that he needed clever trousers to do that, she admitted, watching him as he walked towards her, and reminded herself that all that was behind them.

'Where's the builder?' she asked.

'He had to cancel at the last minute. He's had to go back to London. I tried to ring you, but you'd left.'

She nodded acknowledgement, and wondered where to start. The builder was as good a place as any.

'Perhaps it's just as well he's not here, because I've got something to tell you.' She took a deep breath, and blurted it out. 'I don't want to do Chelsea any more.'

'Fine.' He kept walking, until he was right up to her. 'I don't care about Chelsea. I wanted to talk to you. The builder wasn't coming, it was just an excuse to get you here.'

She blinked, and wondered what on earth he wanted to say that made his mouth go into that grim line and took all the light from his eyes.

'I love you,' he said, without preamble, shocking her into silence. 'I've loved you since I saw you on the train. Probably before that, when I came for drinks and Brian yelled at you and I thought you were going to cry. I wanted to kill him for what he did to you that night. Fortunately fate took it out of my hands and gave me another chance with you, but I thought I'd blown it.'

He looked down at his hands, knotted together, and rammed them into the pockets of his elegantly cut trousers. 'I did everything I could to show you that I loved you, but I didn't want to crowd you, and you made it quite clear on that picnic that you weren't interested in me.

'Then, for some reason you changed your mind and we made love, and I thought now, surely, she'll stay. But you wouldn't. I asked you to stay, but you left anyway—'

'You didn't say you loved me,' she whispered.

'I couldn't. I thought I'd got it all wrong, and pride got in my way—'

He broke off, his eyes filled with tears. 'I had to walk off. I couldn't stand there and watch you drive out of my life like that. I tried to tell myself you were just going home, but I knew it was more than that, and I couldn't bear it.'

'I didn't know what you wanted from me,' she said, her eyes filling. 'I thought you just wanted me to do Chelsea, and your garden, and sleep with you, and entertain your guests—and then you gave me that pen. I would have done it for love—you said that, and you were absolutely right. I would have done—I wanted to.'

'I didn't want you to think I'd taken you for granted,' he said.

She scrubbed a tear off her cheek with her hand, and blinked. 'I just wanted to be a part of it all, I wanted you to take me for granted, I needed it to be the most natural thing in the world that I'd entertain your visitors and help you with the weekend—all the weekends. I didn't want to be treated like a pet mistress—someone that could be bought. I'd been bought before—I wasn't going to let it happen twice.'

She scrubbed her cheeks again, and he handed her a handkerchief. She blew her nose, wiped her mascara all over her face and swore.

He took the mangled handkerchief from her and put it back in his pocket, then tipped her face up to his. 'What are you saying, Georgia?' he asked rawly. 'For God's sake, put me out of my misery. Tell me how you feel.'

She stared at him, at the ravaged eyes, the drawn cheeks, the tightly compressed mouth. 'Oh, Matt, I love you,' she said, and then she was in his arms.

'Thank God,' he whispered, hugging her. 'Thank God.' Releasing her, he led her into the summer house, and she stood dumbstruck in the doorway. On the floor was a quilt, covered with rose petals, and all around the room were strewn flowers from the garden.

'Wait here,' he ordered, and disappeared, coming back a moment later with a bottle of champagne and two tall flutes.

'What's that for?' she asked.

'To celebrate.'

Her heart, so recently soaring, plummeted again. 'Celebrate what?' she asked in a strained voice. 'My acquiescence?'

He looked thunderstruck, then put the bottle down and shook his head. 'I haven't asked you, have I? Damn it, I've forgotten the most important bit!'

And without hesitation, and in his beautifully cut pale trousers, he knelt down on the dirty floor of the summer house and took her hand.

'I love you, Georgia,' he said gruffly. 'I want you with me day and night, for the rest of my life. Marry me. Have my children. Share my life with me. Please—'

'Oh, Matt, I do love you.'

'Georgia, just say yes! For God's sake, please, just say yes!'

She sank down in front of him, her eyes shimmering with tears, and gave him a wobbly smile. 'Yes,' she said. 'Of course I will.'

'Finally!' he said.

He kissed her hungrily, as if he couldn't quite believe she was real, like a condemned man who'd been reprieved. 'I love you so much,' he whispered against her lips. 'I thought I'd lost you for ever, and then Sal came round here and started yelling at me—'

'Sal?' she said, jack-knifing back out of his arms. 'Sal's been here?'

He nodded. 'Why do you think your clothes were missing?'

'She spilt tea—'

'No, she didn't. I told her to take them all away—all except that dress. I love that dress. I wanted to propose to you in that dress, and then, if she was wrong, I would have seen you in it one last time.'

'And if she was right?'

'Then I wanted to undo the buttons one by one, and spread it out, and sprinkle you with rose petals and champagne, and make love to you until there was no room left in your mind for doubt about how I feel for you.'

She smiled, a slow, gentle smile, an age-old smile that took his breath away, and lay back on the quilt.

'So what are we waiting for?' she asked softly.

EPILOGUE

'YOU can't do any more. Stop it. You've got to go.'

'But that geranium—'

'Georgia, it's fine!'

Matt watched her as she looked round at the garden—the summer house, lovingly rebuilt; the floor strewn with rose petals that brought back so many memories; the wild profusion of the roses, all carefully brought on in hot houses and transported here at the peak of perfection, like the other plants; the severe geometry of the knot garden, with the fountain playing in the centre—like a stage set, elaborately created to give the illusion of something real, something that had been like that for centuries.

'It's really beautiful. And it's finished. Everything's cleared up, all the tools are gone—it's done. Come on, you have to rest.'

She laid her hand on her tummy and rubbed absently. Matt shook his head in despair. 'You've overdone it. You're going to have that baby if you don't lie down.'

'Don't be silly, it's not due for two weeks. Do you really think that rose is in the right place?'

'Georgia,' he said, threateningly, and she gave him a teasing smile.

'It's all right, I'll stop. Let's go back to your parents and see the children and sit down.'

'Finally!'

He put her into a taxi outside the Royal Hospital gardens, taking her home before she really did have the

182

baby. It had been a chaotic few weeks, and for the last two, at least, he'd bitterly regretted letting her go on with it once they realised she was pregnant.

Still, it was done, and she seemed all right. Now the judges would walk round and make their decision, and there was nothing more to do until Tuesday.

They watched the Royal Gala Preview on the television on Monday evening—Georgia was too tired to go, and so was he, so they sent his parents instead, and had an early night.

And then in the morning, at half past five, he found Georgia up and dressed and fidgeting. 'What are you doing? Is it the baby?' he asked, suddenly wide awake.

She gave a wry laugh. 'I want to know about the medals,' she said. 'I know we won't have got a gold, but we might have got a bronze, or possibly even a silver or silver-gilt. I just want to know.' She dragged her hair back off her face with impatient fingers and fidgeted again.

He gave up. There was going to be no rest until she had her answer. 'Let's go, then. We'll have breakfast, and make our way there for seven o'clock—and then we'll leave your team there to talk to everyone, and you are coming home again.'

'But it's Members' Day! I have to stay!'

'Not a chance.'

He made her eat, even though he didn't feel hungry himself and could quite understand how she felt, and then they arrived at the gates and were let in on the dot of seven.

Even waddling as she did, he could hardly keep up with her. With a wry grin he jogged a couple of paces and told her to slow down.

'I can't,' she told him firmly. 'I have to see—oh, Matt! We've got something!' She arrived at the picket fence and plucked the card from the top, staring at it with disbelieving eyes.

'Matt, we've got a gold!' she said, and burst into tears.

He felt like crying for her, for all the hard work so amply rewarded, for the dedication, the care and attention she'd given each and every one of her plants, all lovingly tended in the greenhouses at Heveling.

'Well done,' he said, hugging her and fighting back the emotion. 'Clever girl. I knew you could do it.'

She suddenly stiffened in his arms. 'Oh, Matt,' she said, and leant on him, gripping his arms. 'Um—about this baby.'

He looked down at her, at the face pinched with pain and exhaustion, and rolled his eyes. 'What, *now*?'

'Apparently.'

He gave a disbelieving laugh, and scooped her into his arms. 'Come on, we're going to the hospital.'

'But I can't go now!' she wailed, just as her team ran up.

'What's wrong?' Sal asked, scanning her face.

'Nothing,' Matt told them. 'She got a gold, and now she's going to have a baby, so excuse us, please, and hold the fort? I'll be in touch. Bless you.'

He carried her out to the main gate, and there, at the front of the queue, was Mrs Greaves.

'Matt—Georgia! Whatever's happened?' she exclaimed.

'She's got a gold—and she's in labour. Excuse us.'

'Oh, Georgia! Clever girl! I knew you could do it—'

Throwing a grin over his shoulder at the ecstatic Mrs Greaves, he pushed past the gawping crowd, slotted her into a taxi and asked to be taken to the nearest maternity unit.

'Fairly fast, I think, unless you're a midwife?' he added, watching Georgia's face.

'No worries, mate,' the taxi driver said. An Australian. Great. Let's hope he knows the way, Matt thought with a touch of hysteria.

He did. They pulled up outside the hospital, Georgia was put into a wheelchair and whisked into a lift, and twenty minutes later he was a father.

Just like that, without any crises or dramas or complications, a squalling, infuriated little person came into the world and was greeted placidly by her incredibly clever and wonderful mother.

'Congratulations, Mrs Fraser,' the midwife said, beaming. 'You've got a daughter.'

Matt felt tears clog his throat. 'Well done,' he said, bending over and hugging his wife carefully. The baby, slippery and bellowing with indignation, lay on the soft cradle of her abdomen, and her hands were stroking her back lovingly. He touched her with his fingers, marvelling in the softness of the skin, the tiny perfection that was his child.

He stood there pole-axed for a few more minutes while the nitty-gritty of the tidying up was done, and then they handed the baby to him while they moved Georgia into a quiet little room, popped her into a freshly made bed and settled her.

Matt sat down in the nearest chair. He was terrified he'd drop the baby. She was so small, so perfect and fragile and astonishingly beautiful. Well, in fact she was a wrinkled little prune of a thing, if he was honest, but he thought he'd never seen anything more wonderful in his life.

He looked at Georgia, her face serene, the birth forgotten, and thought she was the cleverest, most beautiful woman in the world. His pride was threatening to choke him, and he gulped.

'All right?' she said softly.

He nodded. 'Yes. Just—'

'I know.' She reached out a hand and caressed the soft golden down of the baby's head. 'What are we going to call her?'

'Any preference?'

She shook her head. 'No. I thought I'd ask you. I've been too busy to think about it. We could call her Rose—after all, she was conceived on a bed of rose petals in the summer house—or Veronica, in view of her hasty arrival. The common name for the plant is speedwell.'

'How appropriate,' he said with a chuckle.

Georgia smiled. 'So, come on, you choose. She's your daughter, too.'

And Matt, who was at the end of his tether, grinned and said, 'Anything but Chelsea!'

Romance is just one click away!

love scopes

➢ Find out all about your guy in the Men of the Zodiac area.

➢ Get your daily horoscope.

➢ Take a look at our Passionscopes, Lovescopes, Birthday Scopes and more!

join Heart-to-Heart, our interactive community

➢ Talk with Harlequin authors!

➢ Meet other readers and chat with other members.

➢ Join the discussion forums and post messages on our message boards.

romantic ideas

➢ Get scrumptious meal ideas in the Romantic Recipes area!

➢ Check out the Daily Love Dose to get romantic ideas and suggestions.

Visit us online at

www.eHarlequin.com

on Women.com Networks

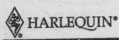

HARLEQUIN®

Harlequin Romance®

Coming Next Month

#3607 THE BRIDESMAID'S WEDDING Margaret Way
When Ally Kinross and Rafe Cameron meet again at her brother's wedding, the attraction between them is as powerful as ever. But their love affair six years ago ended unhappily, and this time Rafe is determined not to get hurt....

Legends of the Outback

#3608 WIFE ON APPROVAL Leigh Michaels
Paige was shocked to see Austin again. It was seven years since she'd called him "husband"—now he was only a client! Except he wanted to give their marriage another try...or did he just want a mother for the little girl now in his care?

Hiring Ms. Right

#3609 THE BOSS'S BRIDE Emma Richmond
Claris was Adam Turmaine's assistant, but her job description had temporarily changed. And if being a stand-in mom was demanding, then living with her boss was equally so—even if he was irresistibly attractive....

Marrying the Boss

#3610 PROJECT: DADDY Patricia Knoll
Paris Barbour could see that Mac Weston adored the two children who had been unexpectedly left in his care—he just didn't know how to show it! As the new nanny, she was determined to help him learn to be a daddy—and possibly a husband, too....

Baby Boom

CNM0500